Official or not, she belonged to him.

Elise turned to look at him. She opened her mouth to say something to Gabriel, but closed it when she saw the look in his eyes. The look of years of yearning.

She let him pull her closer. And when he wrapped his arms around her waist and buried his head into her stomach, she gently hugged his head close stroking his hair with her hands.

She closed her eyes and drew him in. It had been too long since she'd held him like this. Too long since she felt the heat of his body next to hers. There was no retreat this time around. They would finish it here and now.

Books by Vivi Anna

VIVI ANNA

A vixen at heart, Vivi Anna likes to burn up the pages with her original, unique brand of fantasy fiction. Whether it's in the Amazon jungle, an apocalyptic future or the otherworld city of Necropolis, Vivi always writes fast-paced action-adventure with strong independent women that can kick some butt, and dark delicious heroes to kill for.

Once shot at while repossessing a car, Vivi decided that maybe her life needed a change. The first time she picked up a pen and put words to paper, she knew she had found her heart's desire. Within two paragraphs, she realized she could write about getting into all sorts of trouble without suffering any of the consequences.

When Vivi isn't writing, you can find her causing a ruckus at downtown bistros, flea markets or in her own backyard.

A WOLF'S HEART

VIVI ANNA

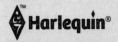
Harlequin®

TORONTO NEW YORK LONDON
AMSTERDAM PARIS SYDNEY HAMBURG
STOCKHOLM ATHENS TOKYO MILAN MADRID
PRAGUE WARSAW BUDAPEST AUCKLAND

Recycling programs
for this product may
not exist in your area.

ISBN-13: 978-0-373-61882-8

A WOLF'S HEART

www.Harlequin.com

Printed in U.S.A.

Dear Reader,

Well, here we are. At the end of the Valorian
Chronicles. I am both saddened and happy about the
event. Sad to be leaving my world and my characters,
but happy that they have been able to be part of your
world for so many years.

I end with Inspector Gabriel Bellmonte. He's a no-
nonsense kind of guy, is all about his job and justice.
An unflappable man—except when it comes to film
star Elise LeRoy. You see, they have a shared past. A
past Gabriel has had a hard time forgetting. So when
he meets up with Elise again, at a crime scene no less,
you can just imagine what's going to happen.

All my best,

Vivi Anna

Chapter 1

Diego grabbed Elise around the waist and pulled her close. "I love you, damn it! I've always loved you. Why don't you love me back?"

Elise nearly cringed. Diego's breath reeked of day-old blood and cheese. For a vampire, he had interesting culinary choices—a combination that made her stomach churn. But being the professional that she was, she spoke her lines with indignation that was not in the least bit faked. "Because you don't deserve my love. You are a petty, insignificant man. And I hate you for what you've done."

Truer words couldn't have been spoken, Elise thought. She pushed out of his hold and moved away from him. But Diego grabbed her arm before she got too far.

"I won't let you go. You belong to me."

Elise stared down at his hand wrapped around her wrist. He was squeezing just a little too hard, a glee-filled look in his eye. Oh, he was a bastard through and through. Why had she ever agreed to this?

"I belong to no man." She lifted her hand and slapped him across the face, hard.

The impact sent him sprawling sideways. "What the hell?" he yelled.

"Cut!" Reginald, the director, exploded out of his chair.

Rubbing his red cheek, Diego stalked over to Elise. "What's your problem? That wasn't in the script."

"I was improvising. Wasn't that what you were doing when you were trying to break my wrist?"

His eyes narrowed, and Elise could see the anger brimming there. She'd always known there was fury inside Diego, but she'd never realized just how much until now. He'd been cast perfectly for the role as the jealous jilted lover bent on revenge.

Reginald stepped in between them, most likely sensing the animosity brewing there. By the shining look in his eyes though, he was thrilled at the opportunity to get it all on film. Diego Martinez and Elise Leroy's tumultuous affair and breakup was legendary.

Elise ground her teeth. She was going to give her agent, Rory, an earful later. She should never have allowed him to talk her into doing this movie. A period film, the script had been beautiful and Elise had fallen in love with the main character, Catherine, but she should've known working with Diego again would result in disaster. Rory had been very persuasive though and in the end she'd agree to take the role.

"I can't work like this, Reggie," Diego whined. "She is constantly messing up the scenes."

"Me? You're the one that changes the lines in the middle of a scene."

"I was merely going with the moment."

She lifted her lips in a sugary smile. "Well, so was I."

Reginald raised his hand. "I'm sorry that she hit you, Diego, but I have to go with Elise on this. It looked fabulous on film." He grinned. "I'm telling you, I can see Oscar on the horizon."

Elise didn't care. She'd been the first Otherworld actress to win an Oscar, so the prospect was lost on her. She'd had her glory. She didn't need more, especially if she had to continue to work with a man she absolutely despised.

"Let's break for lunch, everyone. Back here in

an hour and a half." Reginald clapped his hands together and shuffled off to wherever he went during breaks. Probably to pore over the last shots. Reginald was a meticulous director. That was another reason Elise had agreed to do the film. She had a lot of respect for him and his skills as a director. She liked him as a person, as well. He'd had a long and interesting life that he drew from to make his movies. Rumor was he'd been a drinking buddy of Bram Stoker's. Supposedly he'd been the one to encourage the author's romanticizing of the vampire myth. She was always wondering if Bram had known that Reginald was the very thing he'd been writing about.

Turning, Elise walked off set toward her trailer. This was the third break they'd had today. She'd be surprised if the movie was on schedule, or on budget for that matter. Unfortunately, she couldn't pull out of it at this late date. She'd never breached a contract before and she wasn't about to start now. Diego couldn't run her off the set, if that was what he was trying to pull. It wouldn't surprise her. The man was as petty as they came. But she had to admit, even if she loathed doing it, he could act. He was one of the premier Otherworld actors around. He, too, had won his fair share of accolades and awards. It was just a pity that his talent was wrapped in such a repugnant package.

Lily, her assistant, trailed behind her as Elise

marched across the lot to her trailer. Thankfully, after filming she could escape and go home. Finally, her real home, not a hotel. They'd just returned to Nouveau Monde from a six-month shoot in Paris. It wasn't that Elise didn't like the City of Love, she did, enormously; she'd simply had enough of being away from her own environment. She wanted desperately to curl up in her big canopied bed and sleep for the rest of the day.

Glancing up at the sun glaring down at her, she wondered if that was just her vampire side speaking. Although ultraviolet rays weren't damaging to her, as they were to full-blooded vampires, they did at times make her wish for a comfy place to bed down for a few hours. Putting a hand up to hide her yawn, Elise stepped up to her trailer, opened the door and went in. Lily came in after her. Maybe a hearty meal consisting of very red meat—she had to satisfy her lycan side—and a thirty-minute meditation would do the trick. Being a sangloup, or blood wolf, was sometimes trying, especially since a person had to comply with both genetic quirks.

Sighing, Elise collapsed in the lounger she'd had put in and curled her feet up under her. She set her head on the back and closed her eyes, taking in a few deep, cleansing breaths.

"Can you believe that Diego?" Lily went to the small refrigerator, opened it and came away with a bottle of mineral water. After unscrewing it, she handed it to Elise. "He's such a jerk."

"Yes, I knew that going in." She took a long drink, reveling in the way the cool liquid quenched her dry throat.

"Well, you're a more tolerant woman than I am, that's for sure. I can't stand being around him for more than five minutes."

"I know, Lily. And I appreciate your tolerance." Elise smiled at her young assistant. She was a witch, with incredible skills including organizing and planning. The girl had managed to plan Elise's entire itinerary down to the last minute for the next year, and she didn't need her BlackBerry to track it. She had it all memorized. It was impressive. She'd be lost without her.

Elise was about to tell Lily that, when Lily's cell phone buzzed. She plucked it from her pocket and answered it. "Lily May Jones speaking."

Elise drained the rest of the water and set the bottle on the table next to her. She stretched her body, working out some tense kinks starting to settle. She needed a full-body massage. Maybe she'd get Lily to book her one for later.

"That's unacceptable, Antoine. Ms. Leroy can't wait until the morning." Lily nodded, then smiled. "Thank you, Antoine. You're a doll." She snapped her phone shut and slipped it back into her pocket. "Your massage is booked for eight this evening."

Elise laughed. "I don't know how you do it. But you're always one step ahead of me."

"That's my job. To make sure every need is seen to, even those needs you didn't know you needed."

She laughed even harder. Lily joined in, and they continued until they both had tears running down their cheeks. The tension of the day dissipated like vapor.

When they were able to breathe again, Lily said, "I'm going to find the caterer and see if I can rustle you up some red meat."

"And a spinach salad if he has it."

"Will do. You rest for a bit, and I'll be right back." She opened the door and jumped out of the trailer, shutting the door behind her.

Elise stretched out on the lounger and closed her eyes. She'd take these few minutes to unwind. Never had filming for a movie made her so tense, so out of sorts, but working with Diego was like giving blood and pulling teeth all at the same time. Not a fun way to spend eight months.

Thankfully not all her scenes had been with Diego. He wasn't the hero of the story, but they'd had their fair share of screen time together. Enough that she vowed never to work on another film with him anywhere near it. This would be her last.

The filming in Paris had gone well, exceptionally so despite Diego's efforts to derail her, but they had been long days and nights. She had been happy to be home, back in Nouveau Monde, where she could relax. Once filming was over for the day she could escape to her gated house and lock herself way from everything and everyone.

Although Elise loved her work, she didn't enjoy the other aspects of being a movie star. She guarded her privacy but that wasn't always possible with the paparazzi lurking around every corner. She went to few events, usually to film openings and charity dinners, and preferred to live her day-to-day life as normally as possible. Acting was her job, not her identity. Or at least she tried to make it that way.

But her plan hadn't always been successful. There were some people who refused to separate her as a person from the parts that she played on screen. Such was the curse of being in the limelight all the time.

She opened her eyes just as the door to her trailer opened and Lily stepped in, carrying a covered tray. The heavenly scent of rare beef floated to Elise's nose on a puff of air. She inhaled deeply.

Eagerly, she sat up and pulled the table closer to her. Lily placed the tray on top, and pulled off the lid. "Your dinner is served," she said with a flourish.

"Oh, I nearly forgot." Lily reached into her pocket

and brought out a folded white envelope. She unfolded it and handed it to Elise. "This came for you at the front gate."

Elise took the letter, curious. "What is it?"

"I'm not sure. I guess it arrived by courier."

Elise opened the envelope and the letter slid out. Nerves were now starting to fill her belly. She'd received letters before. Lots of fan mail, but recently she'd been receiving "other" types of letters. Ones she'd been trying to ignore.

She unfolded the white piece of paper, and instantly her heart jumped into her throat.

He'd found her again.

Hands shaking, her fingers couldn't keep hold. The letter fluttered to the floor.

"What is it?" Lily reached down to pick up the letter. "Bad news?"

Lily held the paper up, and Elise's gaze fell to the small dots marking the pristine white. The small red dots that she knew, by scent alone, were blood drops.

Chapter 2

Inspector Gabriel Bellmonte hesitated before getting out of his car. He stared through the windshield at the Nouveau Monde movie studio sign emblazoned in red on the side of the big building in front of him and wondered for the umpteenth time if he could pass this case off to someone else. But the superintendent had made it very clear to him that he, the chief investigator, needed to be on the case. It would be good press for the department and for the superintendent. Besides that, he really didn't have the resources in his department to reassign the case. One of his top investigators, Olena Petrovich, was off on holiday with her newly vamped boyfriend.

Rubbing a hand over his face and sighing, Gabriel opened the door and got out. He went around back, popped the trunk and grabbed his stainless-steel crime-scene kit. It felt like a hundred pounds in his hand as he made his way up to the main door of the studio. He hoped he had the right building. There were over twenty on the studio grounds. The guard at the gate had told him to drive straight through and park on the east side. This was the east side.

He pulled open the gray door and went through. And immediately realized he wasn't in the right building. Not if they were filming in a warehouse overstuffed with all kinds of things. Sofas and lamps, and what looked like painted scenery. The cool thing was he did recognize some of the stuff from films he'd seen.

He made an about-face and went out the door and back to his car. He swiveled around looking for building eight. He would've thought because of his lycan genes he'd never get lost.

"What's the word, Gabe?" Sophie St. Clair, one of his investigators, fell in beside him.

"One of the actors has received a blood-splattered fan letter."

"Who's the actor?"

"Elise Leroy."

Sophie's eyes lit up. "Really? I love her work. Did you see her last movie? It was so good."

"No, I didn't."

Her eyes narrowed. "Everything all right?"

"Yes, I'm fine. Let's just do our jobs." He looked around at the buildings.

She pointed to the big white building on his right. "It's this way."

Without a word, he walked to the building, pretending he'd been waiting for her to show up all along. He grabbed the handle on the door and pulled it open. He went through the opening, Sophie following him in.

It was fairly quiet inside the film stage. Gabriel expected pandemonium considering who the victim was, but what he saw was fairly muted. A few stagehands mingled in the far corner. They appeared to be discussing something about the lighting. Other people, probably assistants and gofers, crossed in front of them, determination making their strides long and quick.

Gabriel moved farther into the building, eyeing everything and everyone as he crossed the floor toward the epicenter of the action—the actual movie set.

When he and Sophie stepped into the light near the soundstage, a big burly lycan with white-blond hair greeted them. "Can I help you?"

Gabriel flashed his badge. "Inspector Gabriel Bellmonte, NMPD."

After his declaration, another man rushed toward him, his hand thrust out. "I'm Reginald Alcott, the director."

Gabriel shook the vampire's hand firmly. "This is Sophie St. Clair." He gestured toward Sophie. The director nodded toward her. "Where is this letter?" Gabriel said.

"In Elise's trailer." He started to walk, assuming that Gabriel and Sophie would follow, which they did. "As you can imagine this has been very upsetting for Elise. So, please, if you can keep your questions to a minimum. I don't want her any more agitated than she already is."

"The show must go on," Sophie commented, unkindly.

The director nodded. "In a manner of speaking, yes."

"The only thing I can promise you is that we will do our jobs fully," Gabriel said.

Reginald looked at him for a moment, likely trying to decide if there was a hidden message in there somewhere. "Good." He gestured toward the long mobile trailer. "Here we are." He knocked on the door.

The door opened and a petite young woman filled the door frame. "No visitors," she growled.

Reginald ducked his head sheepishly. "These people are with the police."

"Oh," she said, and then eyed Gabriel and Sophie, taking their measure. Gabriel felt the telltale spark of magic skimming his body. The little witch was gauging them with her magic. They must've passed, because she said, "Okay. They can come in."

She stepped aside and Gabriel and Sophie entered the trailer. The second he mounted the stairs, Gabriel caught *her* scent. It was remarkable, just as she was, and he'd never forgotten it after all these years. The scent had been imprinted on him long ago.

He moved past the entranceway and spied her in the corner, lounging on a sofa, her long blond hair cascading around her in golden waves. Her gaze fixed on him and he felt the immediate punch in his gut.

She smiled, her little kitten fangs evident between full pink lips. But the smile was sad and it didn't quite reach her emerald eyes. "Hello, Gabriel."

"Hello, Elise."

Sophie gaped at him. "Oh, my God, you know each other? Why didn't you say anything?"

"I imagine it's because Gabriel has put me so far out of his mind he forgets he knows me." Elise took a sip from the liquid in the wineglass she was holding.

Gabriel wasn't going to rise to the bait, although what she'd said wasn't that far from the truth. "Dramatic as always, I see."

"Of course. It's what I get paid for."

He set his kit down on one of the tables and opened it, trying to avoid a verbal sparring match with her. "Can we see the letter, please?" He snapped on latex gloves.

"Lily, could you, please?" Elise nodded toward the petite dynamo who had opened the door. She must be Elise's personal assistant and guard dog.

Lily handed Gabriel an unfolded white piece of paper. He took it and laid it flat on one of the tables on thick plastic sheeting that Sophie had prepared.

Even at first glance, the letter wasn't a typical fan letter. The letters forming the words had been cut from various magazines and periodicals and glued together so that there was no handwriting to analyze.

Then he read the words.

She is gypsy, will not speak to those
Who have not learnt to be content without her;
A jilt, whose ear was never whispered close,
Who thinks they scandal her who talk about her

He looked up at Elise. "Do you recognize this?"
She shook her head.

"Well, it shouldn't be too hard to find. We'll just plug the verse into Google, and we should find it, no problem, if it's from a literary source."

"Maybe it's original," Sophie suggested, reading over Gabriel's shoulder.

"It might be, but I highly doubt it. These types of people are rarely original." He peered down at the red spots near the bottom of the page. It could've been dark red paint or ink, but it wasn't. The odor was unmistakable.

He reached into his kit, took out a large Q-tips and rubbed it over one of the spots, the largest one. Then he retrieved a small plastic bottle of alcohol, the chemical phenolphthalein, and hydrogen peroxide. He dripped two drops of alcohol on the swab, then the phenol and finally the peroxide. The tip turned a purplish-pink.

"Definitely blood present," he said as he held the swab up for Elise to see.

She paled visibly.

"Could be animal blood. We won't know more until we analyze it at the lab." He put the swab into a plastic tube, capped it and labeled the side. He set that into his kit, then took out a plastic bag and slid the letter into it. "We'll fingerprint it at the lab. We'll need the envelope, as well."

Lily handed the plain white envelope to Gabriel. On the front Elise Leroy was printed in printer ink in small capital letters. They might be able to determine what kind of printer had been used.

After putting all the evidence in his kit, he peeled

off the latex gloves. "How many people have handled it?"

Lily put her hand up. "I did, as well as Elise obviously."

"Who else? Where did you get it?"

"From Chuck, who's one of the studio guards at the front gate. He said it came for Elise by a courier."

He glanced at Sophie. "Okay, print Ms. Leroy and Lily, then go with her to the front and talk to this Chuck. Print him and get his statement. We'll need to know the name of the courier company. Call them and get the courier to come down to the station for printing and a statement."

The lycan nodded, and took out her fingerprinting kit and got to work. As she rolled ink onto Elise's fingers, Gabriel tried not to watch. He looked around the trailer instead, trying to get a sense of the woman he had known over fifteen years ago.

She looked much the same. She'd always been devastatingly beautiful. The type of beauty that sometimes is difficult to look at. Because of her vampiric genes, she aged slower, as he did. They were of the same species; both sangloups. They had known each other as children. Grown up together in a sense. But their respective families had been in conflict. For as long as Gabriel could remember, the Bellmontes and the Leroys had been at war. Fighting over territory they'd long ago claimed as their own, a disagreement that had been started by their vampire ancestors and torn their two families apart.

When Sophie was finished, she followed Lily out of the trailer to print the guard and take his statement. Once the door was firmly closed, Gabriel leaned against the kitchenette counter and looked at Elise.

She was busy wiping the black ink off her fingers.

"Are there more, Elise?"

"More what?"

"More letters?"

When she was done cleaning her hand, she tossed the wadded-up tissue in the small garbage can near the kitchenette. "Yes, there are more. I get all kinds of fan mail."

"This goes beyond fan mail, and you know it."

She shrugged and then tossed her hair. It was a typical move for her, especially when she didn't want to talk about something.

"How long have you been getting these?"

She took a sip of her drink. He could see the tremor in her hands. It was subtle, and to another person most likely invisible, but Gabriel was a trained observer, a lycan with fine-tuned senses, and he also knew Elise. "Two years, I guess."

"Two years. And you never thought to tell anyone?"

"They're harmless. Mostly poems."

"Harmless poems written with cutout letters from magazines? Only people with malicious intent think to hide their handwriting with this technique, Elise."

"I never thought to bother anyone with them. I never felt threatened, Gabriel."

He lifted an eyebrow in question. "Until now."

"Yes, until now."

"Did you keep the others?"

She nodded. "They're in a drawer in my office at my house."

"When was the last time you received one?"

"Over six months ago." She set the wineglass back onto the table. "I remember it was right before I flew to Paris for principal shooting on the film."

"You didn't get any while in Paris?"

She shook her head. "No. I actually thought maybe he'd given up."

"And this is the first letter since you've been back?"

She nodded again.

"How long have you been home?"

"Only a few days."

He nodded, and wrote notes in his little notebook that he always carried in his jacket pocket. "Sounds like your fan is a local and knows your schedule."

"Hmm, I guess I never really considered that."

He slid the notebook into his jacket and closed

his crime-scene kit with a snap. "I'll have someone come by and pick up those other letters."

She sat forward on the sofa. "Why don't you come by? We could have tea in the garden."

"No, thanks." He picked up the kit and headed for the door of the trailer. "Someone will be by tomorrow." He opened the door. "We'll keep you apprised of the situation."

"Gabriel?"

He looked over his shoulder at her. She was leaning toward him, biting her bottom lip. He knew that look. It was one of longing and pain.

"I…" She paused, then licked her lips. "It was good to see you again."

He nodded to her and went out the door. At the bottom of the three metal steps, he shut the door behind him, the palm of his hand pressed against it. Closing his eyes, he took in a deep breath, let it out, then dropped his arm and walked away. He had work to do.

Chapter 3

"So, what's she like?"

Gabriel glanced away from the plastic case, where the letter and envelope were being "glued" for fingerprints, and up at Dane, the analyst. "Who?"

"Elise Leroy." The vampire's eyes were bright with curiosity.

"I don't know. I didn't talk to her long."

"Really? I heard you like knew her, knew her."

Gabriel crossed his arms over his chest. "Oh, yeah, where did you hear that?"

"From Sophie."

He shook his head, trying hard not to grind his teeth, and then turned his gaze back to the fingerprinting machine. "So what do we have?"

Wearing latex gloves, Dane opened the box and withdrew the envelope. With his magnifying glass, he examined the loops and swirls of the prints exposed on the white paper. He looked at all of them front and back then set the scope down on the desk.

"Looks like four distinct prints."

Gabriel nodded. That's what he'd thought. According to Lily's statement, four people had touched the envelope—the courier, who they'd tracked down and had come down to give his statement and submit his prints, the studio guard, Lily and Elise.

"How about the letter?"

Dane plucked it from the machine, laid it flat on the desk and examined the dark swirls on the edges of the paper. Gabriel waited patiently as the analyst peered at the paper intently, knowing Dane was the best at what he did. Even if there'd only been smudges, the vampire would be able to decipher them.

"Three different prints."

Gabriel's heart skipped a little. "Are you sure?"

Dane nodded. "Definitely."

"All right. Scan them and run them against what we've pulled from the witnesses. There's going to be one that doesn't match."

The vampire smiled gleefully. "Suspect?"

"I'm hoping."

According to Lily's statement, only she and Elise

had touched the actual letter. So if there was another set of prints, Gabriel had to assume they might belong to the perpetrator.

"Righto, boss man. I'll call you when I get something." Dane saluted him.

With a nod, Gabriel left the analysis room to head back to his office. He had to make sure he got someone to pick up the other letters from Elise's house. They would have to print them all.

He reached his closed office door but before he could open it and escape inside, he heard his name being called.

"Gabriel, if you have a minute."

He glanced toward the superintendent Jakob Weiss as he marched toward Gabriel. Another man strode beside him, his aristocratic face pinched in annoyance.

Gabriel cursed under his breath. He didn't really need a problem like Mayor Benoit Dubois. Since the witch had taken office he'd been constantly in his face, inquiring about this, asking about that. Gabriel had a strong feeling that the man had delusions or boyhood aspirations about being a cop.

"Superintendent." Gabriel nodded at the vampire, then toward the witch. "Mayor."

"We have concerns about the Elise Leroy case," Jakob announced.

Of course. Gabriel mentally sighed. He opened

his office door and beckoned the men in. "Let's talk inside."

It shouldn't have surprised him. Elise had many influential friends. She'd probably called the mayor the second he'd left, telling him about Gabriel's lack of fawning over her.

Gabriel sat behind his desk and gestured to the two visitor chairs. The superintendent sat but the mayor chose to remain standing. Hands clasped behind his back, he wandered through Gabriel's office glancing at the framed commendations on the wall. Gabriel puffed out his chest with the knowledge that there were a hell of a lot of them to look at. Although the mayor and he had several differences of opinions, the witch couldn't deny the number of times Gabriel had saved the lives of citizens of Nouveau Monde.

"This case needs to be handled delicately," Benoit said, his back to Gabriel.

"It's being handled like any other case we get in this office—efficiently and effectively."

Benoit turned to face him. "Well, we both know, Bellmonte, this isn't like any other case." He began walking again. "Elise Leroy is a beloved member of this community, well respected here and in the human community. She's an ambassador of sorts. We would all be greatly upset if any harm came to her."

"Nothing's going to happen to her," Gabriel said. "Trust me, Elise can take care of herself."

"Trust you." Benoit smiled. "That's exactly what I'm going to do."

"My people are working hard on this just like they always do. Sure we're a little short staffed, but it's nothing we can't handle as usual."

Benoit put up his hand as if to swat away Gabriel's protestations. "We're going to give this one some extra attention."

"It doesn't warrant any extra attention, Mayor."

"I understand that your two families have a long history together."

Gabriel's hackles rose, just as if he was being threatened. "I don't see what—"

"It's my job to know everything there is to know about the people who work for me."

"I don't work for you. I work for the city."

Again Benoit waved his hand as if trying to get rid of some foul odor.

"What the mayor is saying, Gabriel, is that because you know Ms. Leroy well, we thought it would be prudent for you to maintain a close connection to her until we get to the bottom of this," Jakob interceded.

"Elise and I aren't exactly friendly, if that's what you think. We haven't been in a long time."

"Regardless, she knows you and we think you'd

be best serving the city and this case if you recon-nected with her."

"What exactly do you want me to do?"

"Be her shadow," Benoit said. "Just until we catch this creep stalking her."

Agitated, Gabriel leaned on his desk. "There is no evidence suggesting the letter writer is a stalker. Could be an overzealous fan."

"And that's why we want someone with Ms. Leroy at all times—so it doesn't turn into a stalker case."

Gabriel sighed. "Fine, if you want to assign a bodyguard to her, go ahead, but it's not going to be me. I have more important things to do than be some starlet's babysitter."

"The decision's already been made," Benoit said. "Your other cases have been reassigned to Maria Ser-rano—she's more than capable of handling them."

"I don't disagree that Maria is a skilled investiga-tor and good administrator. That isn't the point."

"What is?" Benoit asked.

"Doing my job. I'm an investigator and a damn good one. I've run this office for several years and my team has solved more cases than my predeces-sor. That's a testament to how I run the office and I'm not going to forgo that so I can 'look after' one victim on her whim." He was breathing hard by the time he finished his tirade. Usually cool and calm,

Gabriel found his blood pumping through his veins and his heart hammering.

He could feel the beast beating on his insides to come out and play. It had been too long since he'd shifted into his wolf form. Benoit had picked a terrible time to push him. The mayor didn't want to meet his beast, especially since it was amped up by his vampiric genetics. Sometimes being a sangloup was more a curse than a blessing.

Jakob stood, almost as if trying to place himself between Gabriel and Benoit. The superintendent had worked with Gabriel long enough to read the signs. "No one is disputing your amazing work, Gabriel. You are an asset to this office and to the city."

"But?" Gabriel all but growled.

"We think it prudent that you be charged with Ms. Leroy's safety. It is in the interests of everyone involved that she remains protected and happy."

"Sounds like I don't have a choice."

Benoit smiled, but it didn't make Gabriel feel happy. "We all have choices." He lifted one eyebrow toward Jakob then turned on his heel to leave. "I'll inform Ms. Leroy's agent that everything is in order."

The moment the mayor left, Jakob sighed. He ran a hand over his weathered and sunk-in face. One of his investigators once told Gabriel that he thought the superintendent looked like Bela Lugosi. He had to admit there was a resemblance.

"I'm sorry, Gabriel."

He was surprised at the apology. The superintendent usually didn't acknowledge any weakness. His apology told Gabriel that he had no power in this situation, which would've been a first in the many years they've worked together.

He went on before Gabriel could comment. "Think of it as some well-needed time off. You haven't taken a vacation in a long time. Actually, I can't even remember you *ever* taking a holiday."

"This will be far from relaxing, Superintendent, I assure you."

"Well, you'll find something to enjoy about spending your time with the world-famous Elise Leroy. She's a charming woman, and I'm sure you'll be waited on by her people for the entire time. It'll be like being at a luxury spa."

I highly doubt it. He didn't say it out loud, as he didn't want the superintendent to know just how much this assignment bothered him on both a professional level and a personal one. Being around Elise for an extended period of time was going to be one of the hardest things he'd ever have to do.

"Keep me informed about the situation." With a final nod, Jakob exited Gabriel's office, leaving him to seethe.

And seethe he did.

Bolting up from his chair, he paced the office like a caged animal. An angry, frustrated animal that needed release. His blood was boiling so hot that he could barely think. He needed to get out and do something about it now, before he did something foolish.

He marched out of his office, slammed the door behind him and stalked down the corridor to the front doors. As he passed various people on his way, they pressed themselves against the walls, obviously sensing Gabriel's foul mood. By the wide-eyed expressions on most faces, they were probably shocked to see him this way. He was known to be a very cool cucumber.

Sophie approached him. She was about the only person that his mood didn't affect. She had a beast of her own that often needed to be coddled.

"You looked pissed. What's up?"

"I'm going out to run," he managed to grunt between clenched teeth.

"Want some company?"

He shook his head and pressed on, pushing through the doors separating the lab from the precinct, crossing the lobby and out the main doors. Thankfully, the Nouveau Monde Police Department had been situated near a park with lots of running room. They had quite a few lycans working for them and they needed a place where they could stretch their wolf legs.

Gabriel found a secluded place behind some trees, shed his clothes, folded them neatly on the ground and dropped to all fours. He took in a deep breath and started to shift.

It was a painful process, but he needed it, welcomed it. Maybe if he could concentrate on the agony of growing and transforming his bones and muscles, he'd forget about having to spend the next however many days with Elise. To him the pain of the shift was the lesser of the two evils. This pain, this ripping, tearing agony, he could handle. The other, he wasn't sure he would survive.

Chapter 4

"Maybe you should pull out of the movie."

Elise shot her agent an aggravated look over the top of her wineglass. "I'll do no such thing, Rory. Not over one little letter. Besides, weren't you the one begging me to do this film, saying it would be the best thing for my career?"

"First off—" he pointed out on his fingers "—I didn't beg you. I don't beg. I don't need to. You eventually saw that I was right about working with Reginald. And secondly, this letter— It had bloodstains on it, Elise."

"I'm not going to be scared out of doing a film. I have never in my whole career pulled out of a movie.

I don't make promises that I don't plan on keeping." She took another sip of wine and turned her head to gaze out over the expanse of her backyard. That was the reason she had bought the house…for its two acres of land. She inhaled the scent of azalea and tried to remain calm. Sometimes her agent aggravated her, especially now that he'd gone behind her back and tried to strong-arm the police on her behalf. "Besides, we don't know for sure that it's human blood. It could be animal."

Rory snorted. "Do you think that really matters? Blood is blood, and the last place it should be is on a supposed fan letter."

Rory was right, of course, but Elise didn't want to admit it. Ultimately, she didn't want to face the fact that the delivery of the letter had freaked her out. Her hands hadn't stopped shaking for hours after receiving it. Lily had had to shake her to stop her teeth from chattering. And the wine she was holding was her fifth drink of the day and she still didn't feel completely calm.

But she wouldn't tell this to Rory. He was a great agent and had been with her for almost ten years, pretty much since the beginning of her rise to fame. But she didn't share things with him. She didn't share much with anyone, for that matter. Lily was the closest she had to a confidante, and even then she kept most of her feelings to herself. She'd firmly shut and locked the door to her inner self, tossing the key into the darkest, deepest part of her.

Unfortunately, seeing Gabriel again brought that key up just a little bit closer. Almost too near to the surface. It was too tempting to grasp it and unlock her heart, again.

"Elise, are you listening to me?"

She swung her gaze back to Rory. "Probably not. What were you saying?"

"That I'm going to talk to the studio about extra security on the set."

She frowned. "Please, Rory, that is completely unnecessary. I don't want anyone making a big fuss about this. It's in the hands of the police now. I'm sure they will take care of it."

"We're handling it as best as we can."

Elise nearly jumped out of her chair at the sound of the voice. Startled, she set her hand to her chest. Her heart thumped underneath her palm, mostly from fear, but also with pleasure she couldn't deny.

"Inspector Bellmonte. I wasn't expecting to see you again so soon."

Carrying a metal case, Gabriel crossed the patio toward where she was sitting, Lily behind him wringing her hands. "I'm so sorry, Elise, but he insisted that he be let in unannounced."

"It's fine, Lily." She set down her glass on the table, aware that her hand trembled a little as he neared. She was surprised at the reaction. She thought she'd gotten past it, past him. "Rory, this is Inspector Gabriel Bellmonte of the NMPD." She gestured to her agent. "Inspector, this is my agent, Rory Langford."

Rory stood and approached him. The two men shook hands, although from the look on Gabriel's face, he would've sooner torn Rory's throat out than take his hand.

"It's good to know that the police are taking the matter seriously," Rory said after their brief handshake.

"We always take these types of matters seriously, Mr. Langford. Ms. Leroy's case is no different."

He looked right at her when he spoke, as if the last few words were just for her benefit.

Rory smiled, as if oblivious to the angry emotional waves coming from Gabriel. "Well, after this, maybe we can hook you up with a few autographed pictures for your wall. I bet the boys at the station would love that."

"That won't be necessary."

He'd moved closer to where she still sat, at the edge of the patio near the flower garden that she loved so much, but not any closer. She didn't think Gabriel was one for nervousness, but she sensed that was how he was feeling. "Would you care to sit, Inspector?"

He shook his head. "I need to ask you a few more questions, and I need those other letters."

"Of course." She stood, setting the blanket she'd had on her lap onto the chair.

"What other letters?" Rory looked from Gabriel to her. "I wasn't aware of any other letters."

"I didn't want to worry you, Rory." She walked past him and Gabriel to go back into the house. Rory followed close behind her, Gabriel trailing them both. Lily marched beside her, ever the protector.

"Well, I'm worried, Elise."

When she reached the closed door to her office, she turned to face Rory. "Don't be. I have it all under control."

He eyed her, something different in his gaze. "Somehow I don't believe that."

"When have I ever not been able to handle something? In all the years you've known me, when have I ever asked for help or whined about some problem?"

"Never."

"Then why would this situation be any different?"

"Because it is, Elise. This isn't some hard-to-handle actor trying to cause problems on the set, or bad press, or the paparazzi chasing you down the street when you're having a bad hair day. This is…"

She put her hand on his shoulder to soothe him. "It's nothing, Rory. Nothing but an annoyance that

I have every confidence the police will solve." He reached up and laid his hand on top of hers. It surprised her a little and she pulled her hand loose, patted him twice and then dropped her hand. "I'll call you tomorrow, okay?"

Rory glanced to the side at Gabriel, who was leaning against the wall, then back to her. "I think I should stay."

"That won't be necessary. Really. Go home. I'll call you tomorrow."

With a final glance at Gabriel, Rory said his goodbyes and left.

Elise opened the office door, gesturing for Gabriel to enter. He did, albeit reluctantly. Lily fluttered in, as well.

"Lily, could you get us some coffee? Both black." She glanced at Gabriel. "You take it black still, right?"

He nodded.

"Sure." The witch left the office in a cloud of her usual swirling energy.

Then it was just Elise and Gabriel in the office. Although she wanted to see him alone, she wasn't sure if it was the most prudent of actions. By his edgy expression, Elise didn't think he desired the same. His look of contempt was enough to put her back up.

"I don't remember you this cold before. You were always standoffish but never unfeeling."

"Things change."

"Yes, they certainly do." She sat on the chair behind her desk and, taking the key from her slacks pocket, unlocked one of the drawers of her desk. She slid it open and grabbed the tied bundle of letters that she'd received over the years, all seemingly from the same person. She held them up for Gabriel to see.

"Give me a second," he said before opening up the metal case he'd been carrying. He took out a pair of latex gloves, snapped them on and then, leaning forward, took the letters from her.

He sat back in the chair and slid one of the envelopes out, then the letter. He unfolded it to read it. When he was done, he looked up at her. She had to admit she was happy to see concern in his eyes.

"Are they all like this?"

She nodded. "I started getting them a couple of years ago."

"How often do you get them?"

"One a month, I suppose. But only when I'm in town. If I'm out on location, I don't receive them."

He nodded as if that made total sense to him. "And you never thought to mention these to anyone? Not your assistant? Not your agent?"

"I handled it."

He slid the bundle into a big plastic bag and sealed it. "Well, I see that hasn't changed."

"What do you mean?"

He wrote the date, time and place on the bag, and put it into his case. "The fact that you always think you can handle everything, however big or small. That you don't need anyone's help or advice or anything."

And just like that, they were catapulted back fifteen years. Back to the same conversation that had ultimately ended any chance of them having a relationship.

"This is old news, isn't it?" She didn't mean to sound angry but she couldn't keep the bitterness out of her voice.

He stared at her for a few moments, as if trying to decide something. Then he looked away, dismissing the thought just as quickly as he had considered it.

"You're right." He snapped his case closed, peeled off his gloves and tossed them into his pants pocket. He stood and picked up the case. "I'll take these and get the technicians to start checking for fingerprints. If I have any more questions, I'll call."

He was in the doorway when Elise said, "I know my agent called your boss. I know he told you to shadow me."

Gabriel stopped and turned, his face pinched in

annoyance. "And you're telling me you didn't tell him to do that?"

She stood. "No, I didn't. You should know that already. You said five minutes ago that I hadn't changed. Do you really think I would ask for a bodyguard? And that I would ask for you to do it?"

His silence was his answer. He nodded. "I'll see you tomorrow."

She took a step toward him. "I just told you I didn't need a bodyguard."

"I heard you the first time." He turned to leave. But before he did, Elise saw his lips twitch up into an amused smirk.

"You're doing this to aggravate me, aren't you?" she called after him.

She didn't get a response, but she wasn't really expecting one. Gabriel was like that. He always wanted to have the last word.

Chapter 5

The next day Gabriel arrived on the movie set around five-thirty in the morning. Elise was already there, sitting in one of the trailers getting her hair and makeup done. She looked surprised to see him. This seemed to irritate the makeup artist.

"Please don't move, Elise."

"Sorry, Paul," she muttered, then pierced Gabriel with one of her steely gazes. "I told you I didn't need protection."

He shrugged. "Uh-uh. So, where should I stand?"

Lily fluttered up to him. "I'll show you where you can sit and watch the filming, Inspector Bellmonte."

"Thank you." He spared Elise a glance before following Lily out back onto the set and toward a bank of chairs situated far behind the camera setup.

She gestured toward one of the chairs. "You can sit here." She picked up the set of big earphones hanging around one of the arms. "You can listen to what's happening on the set with these if you like."

"I'll pass, thanks." Gabriel didn't sit. Not yet anyway. He wanted to look around the set first and maybe talk to a few people as he did.

"Did you want me to get you a coffee or tea, perhaps?"

"Not right now, thank you, Lily. If I need coffee I'm sure I can get it myself."

"All right." She looked a little put off by his refusal. She probably wasn't used to people in this industry wanting to do things for themselves.

"How long have you worked for Ms. Leroy?"

"About five years now."

"Did you know that she was receiving these letters?"

Lily shook her head, looking sad. "Elise is a very private person. I know only what she tells me."

"Have you noticed anything out of the ordinary in the past year or so? Someone hanging around her house, or the set? Unwanted attention or phone calls from anyone?"

"No, nothing like that."

"Any change in Ms. Leroy's mood or behavior in the past year?"

Her eyebrows came up at that. "The only change I see is in the last two days, but I don't think that has anything to do with the letter."

Gabriel wondered if Lily knew about his and Elise's past relationship. He didn't think so. If Elise was as private as Lily said she was—and Gabriel believed she was—she wouldn't share that information, even if the man from her past showed up unexpectedly.

The area around the camera started to fill up with various people. Someone dressed in clothes from the eighteenth century marched by, his nose in a twist.

"Would someone get me a bottle of O negative?" he bellowed, evidently hoping somebody complied with his demand.

Lily sniffed but made no move to fulfill the request.

Gabriel eyed the man. It was Diego Martinez— actor, philanthropist and all-around jerk about town. Or at least from what Gabriel read in the newspapers. He knew that Diego and Elise had had a tumultuous relationship years ago. Their public breakup had been well publicized. Not that he'd been keeping tabs on Elise's relationships or anything. It was just hard to ignore something like that when it was broadcast on every television station and dredged over in every newspaper and magazine.

"Are Ms. Leroy and Mr. Martinez…?"

"Oh, heavens, no." Lily laughed. "That was over years ago. They can't stand each other."

"And yet, here they are doing this movie together."

"Elise is only doing this film because of the director, Reginald Alcott. She's wanted to work with him for years and years. She wasn't about to let Diego get in the way of that. Besides, Rory thought it was the best thing for her career, and I tend to agree."

Gabriel nodded. "Thank you, Lily. I've taken up enough of your time."

She gave him a small smile then scampered away, back to the makeup-and-hair trailer, he assumed. Once she was gone, he wandered away from the bank of visitor chairs and toward the set. He was hoping for a few minutes with Diego Martinez.

As he approached the vampire, Gabriel noticed that someone had gotten him his bottle of blood, and he was lustily drinking it down. "Mr. Martinez, may I have a few minutes?"

Diego eyed him warily. "Who are you and what do you want? If you want an interview you'll have to speak to my publicist."

Gabriel dug out his wallet and flipped open his badge. "Inspector Bellmonte, with the NMPD."

"You must be here because of the 'letter' Elise received." He air quoted the word *letter*.

"You don't sound too concerned about it."

He shrugged. "It wouldn't surprise me if she sent that letter to herself."

"Really? Why would you say that?"

"Elise is a huge drama queen. She can't survive when the spotlight isn't on her, all the time." Diego didn't meet Gabriel's gaze when he made that statement; instead, he was looking off toward the set. "Now if you'll excuse me. I have work to do."

Gabriel watched Diego stomp away in search of someone to fawn over him, he supposed, and thought the vampire was a self-engrossed idiot. He knew for a fact that Elise was far from a drama queen. She was the opposite. She didn't crave the limelight at all. That was not the reason she pursued an acting career. He still knew that much about her, at least.

Before Gabriel could find someone else to question, Elise came onto the set and it was as if the entire studio fell into a reverent silence. All the cast and crew watched as she moved, floating, it appeared, with the long skirt swishing around her ankles. He had to admit he was just as mesmerized by her. Still mesmerized, he guessed. Because he'd been awestruck by her since they were kids.

So instead of doing his job, he backed up, found a chair and sat down to watch her make movie magic.

* * *

Two hours later, Gabriel's butt was numb and his throat was dry. He desperately needed something to drink. But it had been worth it to watch Elise work. She was stunning. When she was before the camera, she transformed into that character. It was amazing to watch even for a layman who knew nothing about the business and couldn't care less about it.

He slid off the chair and was going to sneak away to grab a drink before anyone could see him, but as if on cue, Elise was beside him.

"Did you enjoy the scene?"

He wanted to say something coy, but instead he spoke the truth. "Yes. You're very talented. I've always enjoyed your films."

She smiled then, and it lit up her beautiful face, as if a lightbulb had been clicked on inside. He had to look away before being sucked into that light, like a moth to a flame.

"I didn't know you'd seen my movies."

He shrugged. "I like to go to the theater once in a while. You know, on a day off."

"I didn't know you took days off, either."

He glanced up at her. She was still smiling at him, and this time there was humor in her gaze. He returned the smile. "It's been known to happen every so often. Yeah, who knew I had a life?"

Elise licked her lips and opened her mouth as if

she wanted to say something then, but changing her mind she lowered her gaze and played with the rings on her fingers. "Have you found anything out?"

He shook his head. "Not much. What's it like working with Diego again?"

"Like hell." She shook her head. "But I think it will be worth it. I think this is going to be a fantastic film. The script was amazing and I just couldn't say no."

"So, you two aren't on good terms at all?"

"You could say that."

"Could I say that there is animosity and possibly hatred?"

Elise frowned. "I wouldn't say hatred. At least not on my part. I don't hate Diego. I just don't like him very much. But he's one hell of an actor. I have to admit that."

He nodded.

She leaned closer to him. He could smell her perfume and the scent of her skin. "You don't think he had anything to do with these letters, do you?"

"Can't say. Anything's possible at this point."

She just nodded, but Gabriel could see the worry on her face. He didn't think she'd ever considered Diego to be the one sending the hate mail. He didn't know if that was the case, but Gabriel had heard the derision in Diego's voice. There was a high level of animosity directed toward Elise. Jealousy certainly, too. Maybe there was still a sense of entitlement there as well, sick and twisted by her leaving him. He wouldn't count Diego out as a suspect.

"Elise, we're ready for you," Reginald called to her.

She waved her hand at him then turned back to Gabriel. "I didn't say thank-you. I know you really don't want to be here and I imagine you probably fought tooth and nail against coming."

Gabriel couldn't help the smile that curved his lips. She knew him too well.

"So." She sighed. "Thank you."

"You're welcome."

She gave him a final nod, and turned to walk back to the main set. Then she stopped and glanced over her shoulder toward him. "So, I'll see you later tonight then?"

"What's tonight? I thought you were done filming around six?"

She lifted one elegant eyebrow. "You'll see."

Chapter 6

And he did see. Unfortunately.

Gabriel fussed with the buttons of his rented tuxedo as he scanned the crowded room for a way to escape.

Lily regarded him from under long black lashes. "Would you quit fidgeting? You look good."

He sniffed at her. He knew he looked out of place, and definitely uncomfortable. He preferred his battered suit jacket and worn jeans to this monkey suit. And he liked wearing his tan fedora every once in a while so he could hide the fact that his hair didn't always behave. He'd slicked it back with a lot of gel for this occasion, but the front was stubborn and curled down onto his forehead.

Before he'd left to come to the party, he battled with it for a half hour then just given up. It didn't really matter what he looked like anyway. He was at the Grand Hotel in a law-enforcement capacity. He was here to make sure Elise was safe. This wasn't a date with the most spectacular woman alive.

They hadn't even come together. He arrived alone, met up with Lily, only because she was watching out for him, and he would do his job and leave by himself. Elise hadn't even arrived yet. He figured it was just like her to be late.

Some would think it was because she liked to make an entrance, to be at the center of attention, but he knew it was because she didn't wear a watch and she didn't much care for time. She'd always said it was a waste to watch time.

"You're not very comfortable in a suit, are you?"

He pulled at the bow tie. "Now, why would you say that?"

Lily laughed and slapped him on the arm. "It baffles me that you two were ever together."

He glanced at her, his hand stilling on his tie. "She told you about us?"

She nodded. "Just briefly. Said it was a long time ago and you were both very different people." She looked him up and down. "You must've been very different then." She laughed again and then squeezed his arm tight. "Oh, here she comes."

There was a murmur through the crowd. It didn't take long to realize the point at which Elise had entered the party. All heads had turned that way.

Gabriel thought he was prepared to see her dressed up, but the reality of her couldn't be planned for. She was stunning in a strapless sheath of sapphire-blue. Her skin was so pale, like smooth flawless marble, against the darkness of the silky fabric. Her long golden hair was pinned up in a smooth sweep, accentuating her delicate neck. It was elegant and beguiling and Gabriel could see the vein pulsing along her jawline. It wasn't often that his vampiric genes came out to play but right now he found he wanted to press his lips to that pulsating vein. Her blood would taste like ambrosia. Gabriel found it very difficult to breathe.

He put a hand to his chest when Elise neared.

She regarded him curiously. "Are you all right, Gabriel?"

"Yes," he managed to say. "I have heartburn. It must've been something I ate."

Her lips twitched a little, as if to stifle a laugh. "You look very nice in that suit."

He straightened his shoulders and met her gaze. "And you look, ah, beautiful."

"Thank you." She lowered her gaze demurely.

It wasn't often that Elise allowed another to take charge. She was usually the aggressor, the alpha in most situations. Just another reason their relationship had failed—her inability to allow him to be the alpha, to be her protector.

Lily cleared her throat. "Um, I'll get you two drinks. I'll be right back."

When she was gone, Elise slid in next to him and placed her hand on his arm. She leaned in to whisper in his ear. "Stroll with me around the room. I have to do my duty at this thing and greet people."

Not wanting her to touch him, but not knowing a way to disengage her hand without looking like an ass, Gabriel nodded and started to walk. He could feel the heat of her body even through the heavy fabric of his suit.

"Why are we here?" he asked quietly.

"It's a charity ball for children. To raise money for the new hospital that will be able to treat all children, both human and Otherworlder."

"I got that part," he said. "But wouldn't it be better, safer, if you weren't making public appearances? At least until we solve this case?"

"I won't let anyone make me a prisoner of fear," she said, then smiled at a passing man. "Good to see you, Günter."

The man, Günter, kissed Elise's cheeks. "You get more beautiful every time we meet."

"Thank you." She smiled, turning on the charm. "I expect a huge donation from you, my friend."

"Of course. I wouldn't dream of disappointing you."

He kissed her cheeks again, bowed his head, then was off.

"That was the German Otherworlder ambassador. He's one of the richest men in Europe."

Gabriel and she continued their way through the party. He watched as she smiled and charmed everyone in the room. Kissing cheeks, shaking hands, air kissing women who seemed to have sticks up their butts. Gabriel was getting annoyed and exhausted just watching it all take place in front of him.

He thanked her for forgoing his introductions. Instinctively, she must've known that he really didn't want to shake hands with anyone at the party. That he preferred to hang in the background and let her play her part. This was one time he didn't mind being her accessory.

After they had made one complete circuit, Lily caught up with them and delivered flutes of champagne. Gabriel held his with polite interest but he didn't drink.

"Don't you get tired of it?" he asked Elise, once Lily had fluttered off again to do whatever she needed to do.

She lifted one eyebrow in answer, and then took a sip of the champagne. "Don't you?"

"I don't know what you mean."

"Being the tough guy. The guy in charge."

He smirked. "Nope."

She laughed and he found that he was actually enjoying himself. It had been a long time since he'd been out with a beautiful woman. A woman who made him feel both comfortable and uneasy at the same time. That was what being with Elise had always been like. Keeping balance on a high wire.

Gabriel took that moment to set his drink down on the nearby bar and roll his shoulders. Usually tense, he was finding that sensation starting to diminish. Maybe it was her laugh that gave him a sense of comfort, familiarity, a reason to let down his guard.

A band set up on a stage in the corner started to play and an area in the middle of the room was instantly cleared for dancers. Elise looked at him and grabbed his arm again.

"Dance with me."

"I don't think so."

"We used to dance together. Don't you remember?"

Yeah, he remembered. They'd been teenagers, hormones raging like wildfire and he spent most of the dance pulling her close and running his hands over her well-formed rear end.

"I remember, but I don't think anyone here wants to watch me fondle your backside."

She laughed again, and then dragged him through the crowd and onto the dance floor. People moved out of their way the second they saw them coming. It was surreal to have everyone in the room watching them. Gabriel suddenly felt very nervous. As if he was under investigation, under inspection. As if every person in the room was taking his measure to see if he was up to Ms. Elise Leroy's standards.

He could've saved them the trouble of trying to figure that out. He didn't measure up in the least. Elise had always been too good for him. Her parents never had a problem letting him know that when he'd been courting her all those years ago.

He set his hand on her waist and held her hand out to the side, trying hard not to pull her close. He wanted to. Desperately. But he fought it by biting down on the inside of his cheek.

They whirled around the floor. Surprisingly, Gabriel didn't step on her feet even once. At one point, he thought he was doing a pretty good job of faking it. That it looked like he knew what he was doing. Until the music slowed a little and Elise pressed in close to his body, running her one hand up to his neck to play with the ends of his hair.

He could hear her heart thumping and the blood rushing through her veins. The scent of her skin and her hair wafted to his nose and he inhaled them both with relish. He'd always loved her smell. He could distinguish it from thousands of others thanks to his lycan olfactory cells.

"I've missed this," Elise muttered, as if only to herself, but he knew it was for his ears.

"What?" His heart thumped harder.

"Connecting with someone. You know, just being me with someone. Someone I don't have to pretend for."

"Yeah, I can imagine how fake all of this is."

She shook her head. "You make it sound distasteful—the work I do, the life I lead."

"That's not what I meant." He sighed, realizing he could never really say what he truly meant with her. His words always ended up in a jumbled mess. "Just that you have a certain persona you have to portray. And not just in your movies."

They twirled around the floor again, in silence. A comfortable one, he noticed. It felt nice to have her in his arms again. He found he could quite easily fall sway to her again and that deep down inside, he wanted to with all his heart.

"Why haven't you come see me? Why have you stayed away for so long? It's not like you haven't known where I've been. You're a detective. You could've easily found me."

Gabriel stumbled a little and almost stepped on her right foot. He looked down at his feet and issued a clumsy apology. "I need some air."

Without waiting for her reply, he left the dance floor and headed for the veranda. He went through the open glass doors to lean on the railing. He took in a few deep breaths then flinched. Elise had moved in to stand beside him. He should've known she'd follow him. Maybe that had been his intention to begin with.

She leaned on the railing and looked off toward the city skyscape. "I've missed you. I didn't realize just how much until I saw you again."

"Why didn't you come see me? It wouldn't have been that hard to find me." It was a juvenile thing to say, but something about the situation had catapulted him back fifteen years to when he was a dumb, foolish teenager head over in heels in love with a girl he had no business loving.

She didn't answer him, probably thinking he was being an ass. He knew he was acting like one.

Damn, he wanted to touch her, run his fingers over her delicate jawline, trace the full rise of her incredible mouth. But he didn't. He squeezed his hands tighter around the railing.

She turned to him. "Have you missed me?"

He sighed. "What do you want me to say?" He turned to her then. "That I think about you almost every day. That I have all your films on DVD and I watch them at least once a month. That I can't run in Chamberlain Park anymore, because it hurts to remember our runs together there. Is that what you want to know?"

She covered his hand with hers. "I didn't know."

Disgusted with himself for revealing his emotions, Gabriel tugged his hand away from hers. "It doesn't matter. Water under the bridge. After we've solved your case, you can move on again with your life and leave me in the past where I belong." Distancing himself from the railing and from Elise, he glanced at his watch. "I'm going to walk you to your car now." He offered her his arm.

She opened her mouth, perhaps to argue or respond to his rushed confession, but instead she nodded and took his offered arm.

As they exited the party, Elise kissing people and shaking hands along the way, Gabriel tried to get a hold of himself. He hadn't meant to spew all that to her. He had just meant to say yes, he'd missed her, as well. But anger and resentment and loss had suddenly constricted tightly within him, and he needed to rid himself of it. Probably not the best way to go, but he couldn't take it back. He'd just try to forget he'd said anything at all.

He held the door for her and they left the hotel to find her car. She pointed to the side of the street where she said her driver had been told to wait. But as they approached the long black sedan, Gabriel sensed something was wrong.

First of all, her driver was nowhere to be found.

And second, something had been scratched into the black paint of the car. One word. *Bitch.*

Elise's letter writer had just crossed the line from annoying obsession to threatening stalker.

Chapter 7

Within minutes, the paparazzi were snapping pictures of Elise in front of the vandalized car. She didn't even have time to fully comprehend the situation before Gabriel had wrapped her in his arms and escorted her to his official vehicle. He opened the back door for her, helped her inside and then shut it again.

He stood just outside her door, keeping the press back, as he flipped open his cell phone and made a call. She imagined he was phoning his people. Investigators to come and find out how her car had come to be vandalized, right in front of the most prestigious hotel in Nouveau Monde. And where the hell was her driver? Wasn't that what she paid him for? To protect her vehicle? To be there when she needed him to be?

Digging into her purse, Elise came away with her own phone, flipped it open and dialed her driver's number. She got his voice mail. She left a very direct, very simple text message. You're fired.

He'd probably slipped away thinking he could talk with the other drivers for a while, likely smoke a cigarette or have a drink, before he had to be back at the car for her arrival. She hadn't wanted to use a different driver this evening, but her usual man had been unavailable. She was so angry she could've crushed her cell phone in her bare hand.

Anger was good. Anger she could deal with. It was the other emotion threatening to take over that she didn't want to deal with. Fear. It had a way of paralyzing a person and Elise refused to bow down to it.

Her door opened again, and Gabriel stuck his head in. "I'm going to have someone drive you home while I wait for my team."

She grabbed his hand. "Can you take me?"

"I have to wait for my team."

"That's fine. I can wait."

He gestured to the flashing cameras. "What about them?"

"I'm sure a man like you can do something about that."

He smiled at her, and she felt a little of her anxiety and fear lift. Gabriel had always made her feel safe and secure just by looking at her in a certain way.

"Done. Hang tight." He shut the door.

Sighing, she closed her eyes and rested her head on the back of the seat. She couldn't believe this was happening. She'd just wanted to come to the event, dance a little, drink a little, shake hands and raise money for her favorite charity. But now she had to deal with someone vandalizing her car. And it wasn't just any vandal, she knew. This was a personal attack on her. This was by someone who harbored strong feelings about her.

A knock on the window startled her enough to open her eyes. Diego was staring in at her. She rolled down the window.

"What are you doing here?" she asked.

"I heard what happened."

"No, what are you doing here?" She gestured to the hotel. "I didn't think you were one for charities."

"I'm not usually, but I thought it would be good press."

She sighed wearily. "Of course you did."

He shrugged. "Anyway, I was just making sure you were all right."

"Since when did you care?"

"I've always cared, Elise." A hundred cameras flashed as Diego delivered his line loudly and with gusto.

If they hadn't been surrounded by the press, Elise would've gotten out of the vehicle and told him exactly where he could shove his devoted attitude.

Instead she plastered on a saccharine smile and said, "I do appreciate your concern, Diego, but you can rest assured I am one-hundred-percent fine."

He glanced over at his young big-breasted date for the evening. She was primping and pouting for the cameras. "Well, that eases my mind. Have a great rest of the evening, Elise. I'll see you tomorrow on the set."

She rolled up the window so she didn't have to hear him play the good, decent guy to the paparazzi. Anyone with half a brain knew that was all an act. What was Diego doing here anyway? He didn't usually attend charity events, especially not her charity events. Unless he was using the extra press about her letter to get in more pictures and articles. It wouldn't surprise her in the least. Diego was a media whore. He thrived on the attention.

If she could go back three years ago, she would've heeded her agent's warnings about him and never have gotten involved with the vampire. Those four months had been the biggest mistake of her life.

She was about to shut her eyes and lean her head

back again, when the front driver's side door opened and Gabriel jumped in.

"Ready to go?" He glanced at her in the backseat.

"Very."

The drive to her home was quick and quiet, which suited her fine. She was too tired and mentally worn-out to make polite conversation. She didn't know what to say anyway. Talking about the weather seemed trite and inconsequential compared to this evening's events.

When Gabriel pulled up to the locked gate, he made sure she could reach the intercom from the backseat. She rolled down the window and punched in her pass code on the alarm keypad. The black box beeped and the tall iron gates slowly spread open. Gabriel drove the car through and parked in front of the main door. He got out of the vehicle, came around to the side and opened her door for her. He reached in with his hand.

She took the offer and slid out. When she was standing, he dropped her hand and shut the door. She wished he would've continued to hold her hand, just for a little while. Just until her body would stop shaking.

Gabriel walked her to the door. "Do you want me to call someone to come stay with you? I could have an officer here within fifteen minutes."

"Could you stay?" she said in a rush. "I know it's asking a lot from you, considering."

He looked at her for a moment. She wasn't sure what he was looking for. At one time she had always been able to guess what Gabriel was thinking, but now he was so guarded she couldn't be sure of anything. After what seemed like forever, he nodded and followed her into the house.

She led him to the library. It was her favorite room in the house. It was cozy and warm, packed floor to ceiling with books, and it had always reminded her of her childhood home. She gestured toward the long leather sofa near the fireplace. "I need to change."

He nodded.

"I could pour you a drink, if you like?" She started for the small bar in the corner.

"Go and change, Elise. I can pour my own drink if I need it."

She nodded and retreated to her bedroom. She quickly shed her dress, hung it back up in her closet, and donned a long emerald-green silk robe she'd bought in Japan. She went into her bathroom, unpinned her hair, brushed it out and quickly washed her face. After sliding on silk slippers, she returned to the library.

Gabriel was sitting on the sofa with a short glass of what looked to be brandy in his hand. When she approached, he lifted the other glass on the table and handed it to her.

"I thought you would need this."

Sipping the brandy, she sat beside him on the sofa, curling her legs up under her. "Thank you." She drank all of the alcohol then set the glass onto the table. Sighing, she leaned her head back onto the sofa cushions and looked at Gabriel. He was busy staring at anything but her, sipping his drink. "I'm sorry I got you involved in this."

"It's my job, Elise. It has nothing to do with you."

"Oh, well, I see."

Sighing, Gabriel drained the rest of the brandy and set the glass onto the table with an audible clunk. "Not everything is about you."

"Oh, I realize that."

He turned toward her. "No, I don't think you do."

They stared at each other. The heat in the room seemed to intensify exponentially. Elise could feel the hum of his power skimming the surface of her skin and it made her quiver with need. She missed his intensity. She missed how he made her feel, all keyed up and on edge. Like anything could and would happen with him around.

Unfurling her legs, she sat up, leaning closer to him. His scent filled her nose and she nearly sighed with desire. Just his smell alone could ignite all her senses. Licking her lips, she moved even closer to him, excited that he didn't pull away. "Are we still talking about the case?" she murmured.

"I don't know." His hand snaked across the sofa cushions and fell onto her thigh. The second he touched her she felt a jolt of pleasure charge up her body. She could barely contain herself. She wanted nothing more than to breach the distance between them and claim his mouth, claim him.

"It's hot in here," she announced stupidly.

"Yes, it is." The pupils in his eyes dilated and his nostrils flared.

But before she could lean any closer and capture his lips with hers, Lily burst into the room, like a charged butterfly.

"Oh, my God, I can't believe it." She crossed the room in four steps and wrapped her arms around Elise. "I'm so sorry I wasn't there."

She patted the girl's back. "It's all right, Lily. I'm fine. Gabriel brought me home."

Lily pulled back and looked at Gabriel. "Thank God for you, Inspector Bellmonte."

"Yeah." He stood and smoothed the wrinkles in his pants. "And now that you're here, I'm heading back to the crime scene."

Elise stood, too, not wanting the magic to dissipate, not when they were so close to talking about the horrible distance between them. A distance filled with pain and sorrow, but also love and passion. She wanted to remind him of that latter part.

"I'll walk you out."

"I'm fine, Elise. I'm sure I can find my way." With a curt nod, he made his way around the sofa and toward the door.

"I'll see you tomorrow on the set?" she asked, hoping she didn't sound desperate.

"Yeah, you'll see me tomorrow." And with that he left.

Lily continued to fuss over her, but she managed to tune it out. The only thing she could clearly hear was the thumping of her heart. It hurt, but it was a pain she welcomed. She'd gone too long feeling numb. Gabriel had awakened her and she planned on staying that way.

Chapter 8

As Gabriel watched the scene being filmed from the corner of the soundstage, he hid a yawn behind his hand. He'd managed maybe two hours of sleep last night. After leaving Elise's he'd returned to the crime scene. He knew he didn't have to, as his team was exemplenary at what they did, but he felt a need to be directly involved.

He couldn't deny that seeing that word scratched into Elise's vehicle had angered him. He wanted someone to pay for causing her anguish. His natural protective traits were kicking in. Elise did that to him. Made him want to do everything he possibly could to keep her safe and secure. And deep down, he also desired to make her happy.

It was a feeling he couldn't shake. He'd been trying—thought he had succeeded—to bury that need deep in his heart, only to have it resurface now. Seeing her again had brought up all kinds of emotions. Emotions he wasn't willing or able to deal with. Not now at least. He had to be completely focused on the job at hand.

So far, they had nothing to go on. There'd been no witnesses to the vandalism. Gabriel found that hard to believe when the car had been in front of a busy hotel the entire time. They also hadn't managed to find the driver. After some investigation though, Gabriel discovered that the driver, a lycan, had a warrant out for his arrest. So it was possible he'd skipped town after everything went down. Elise told him that she'd left a message on the guy's phone to tell him he was fired. What bothered him the most though was he couldn't ascertain who had hired the driver.

One of the other limo drivers gave a statement that he saw Elise's driver get out of the vehicle and jog across the street, and he didn't see him return. But Gabriel wasn't sure how reliable the guy was, because after that he'd admitted that he'd gone around back with some other staff, other drivers and hotel staff, to smoke and play some cards. After talking to a few more people, it appeared that no one had been standing at the front of the hotel when the vandalism occurred.

So, as far as Gabriel was concerned, the vandal could've been anyone at the party. Guests were coming and going all evening. Anyone could've had the opportunity. And because of that, Gabriel had been busy cross-referencing the party guest list with anyone who might have some grudge against Elise.

Unfortunately, he discovered that list was going to be long.

The famous, rich and successful never failed to have a number of people who held some sort of grudge. Jealousy, feigned snubs, real snubs, all of these could be motive enough for a stalker.

He yawned again just as Lily approached him. She smiled, holding out a foam cup of steaming coffee. "You look like you need this."

He took the drink. "Thank you." He sipped the hot liquid, impressed that the witch always seemed to know what was going on, and who needed something. This made him think that out of everyone in Elise's life, she would know pretty much everything.

He eyed her curiously as he drank the strong coffee. Her gaze was glued to the set, where Elise and Diego were playing out a big important scene. According to one of the grips he'd talked to earlier, this scene was the climax of the film. By the way Lily seemed mesmerized by Elise, Gabriel had to wonder if there was more there than just employer loyalty.

"How's Elise doing?" he asked her.

"She's okay. Tired mostly." She smiled. "But she's a consummate professional, so it won't affect her performance. I'm not sure anything could bother her enough that it would affect her acting." Did he detect a note of disapproval in her voice?

"Elise has always been driven."

Lily snorted. "You could say that."

"It sounds like you don't approve."

She shook her head, looking at him with wide eyes. "No, it's not that. I respect her ambition to always be the best. It's just hard sometimes to live up to, you know."

He nodded. He did indeed know all about that. "I imagine that must make it difficult to work for her, then."

"Oh, goodness, no. Elise is amazing to work for. I wouldn't want to work for anyone else. She's kind and caring. And I—"

"Love her."

She peered at him with a strange expression. "I was going to say respect her. But in a way I guess I do love her. I know I'd do anything for her."

Nodding, he drank the rest of his coffee. "I was surprised that you weren't there by Elise's side last night. That you didn't show up at the house until much later."

She glared at him. It was a very unpleasant look and he was surprised by its vehemence. It was obvious the witch had more to her than just bubbling energy. Maybe there was more than one actress here in this partnership.

"I had business to attend to."

"For Elise?"

"Yes, for Elise." She crushed the foam cup she was holding and tossed it into the garbage can behind him. "I can give you names and numbers if you like."

"I don't think that's necessary." He smiled and also tossed his empty cup into the trash bin. "Right now."

"If you'll excuse me, I have more work to do." She stomped away from him, her heels making quite a racket as she did.

He digested everything she'd said and he made a mental note to watch her more. She was hiding something. It might be no more than she was using Elise's private hairdresser as her own, but it was something. If it was harming Elise in some way, then Gabriel would find out.

Needing to stretch his legs, he walked around the soundstage, always mindful he didn't venture too close to the set. He didn't want to get in the way. But as he crossed behind the director, he risked a peek at the scene. It appeared to be nearing the climax. From the snippets of dialogue he heard, Elise's and Diego's characters were having it out. Lots of screaming and curse words.

He had to admit it was difficult to watch Diego yell at Elise, difficult to hear him call her foul names. Although Gabriel knew it was an act, that they were playing parts, the urge to rip out Diego's throat surged through him. At one point, he had to dig his nails into the palms of his hands to stop from rushing the stage and going to her rescue.

He knew she'd berate him for it. Elise was no weak wallflower, and she'd be the first to tell him that. She didn't need any rescuing, thank you very much. Hadn't she told him that very thing all those years ago when he thought he was coming to her rescue?

His stomach rumbled, reminding him he hadn't had breakfast yet. He was about to cross the floor and check out the spread of food on the other side of the stage, when something gave him pause.

It was nothing concrete. Nothing that he could immediately put his finger on. It wasn't a noise or something he spied out of his peripheral vision. No, it was more a feeling. Like something ominous was about to happen. The hair on his arms and the back of his neck stirred to attention. He had an urge to suppress a shiver.

He glanced up at the high ceiling on the sound-stage above the set. Was there an open shaft up there? A hole where a cool breeze was blowing in? Something like that may have given him the creeping sensation. He couldn't see anything but wires and hooks, and a giant lighting apparatus. Nothing out of the ordinary.

But he still couldn't shake the feeling.

He moved closer to the set, standing not far behind the director in his chair. The cameraman was up on a lift, filming the intense scene. Gabriel's gaze settled onto the set, onto Elise and Diego. He watched as they moved around the set, Diego pursuing Elise, the film's final showdown between the heroine and the villain.

He knew Elise would have a mark, a spot designated on the set's floor to indicate where she needed to end up for the camera to zoom in on her. Moving closer, Gabriel found that sticker, outlined in yellow. Then he glanced up above it.

Elise was almost there. Almost at her marker, preparing for the big close-up, the huge emotional moment of the movie. He couldn't wait any longer. It had to be now.

Gabriel rushed toward the set, pushing chairs and equipment out of his way. There were shouts of indignation and protestation in his wake, but he kept moving. Elise was his number-one goal. He couldn't fail.

By now, Reginald the director was calling, *"Cut, cut, cut!"* And the rest of the crew realized something was going on.

Gabriel pressed on, gaining speed. As he stepped onto the set, he leaped over the sofa that was in his way and continued forward. Elise was turning now, toward him, her eyes wide, angry words forming in protest. But she didn't get the chance to say anything.

He pushed her hard across the set. Hard enough to send her sprawling at least twenty feet. He didn't have to worry about Diego, though. The vampire was already halfway across the soundstage.

It was then his foot landed on the yellow marker on the floor and the ceiling right above him came crashing down. Gabriel had only seconds to brace for the impact.

He raised his hands to stop a thousand pounds of metal and plaster from landing on top of him. But it proved pointless. It landed right on top of him. A thin metal rod pierced his leg. Pain, immediate and sharp, surged through him like a dark icy wave of water. And that's when everything went black.

Chapter 9

Elise brushed the stray dark hairs from Gabriel's brow. She'd been sitting in his hospital room for the past three hours, battling the urge to kiss his cheek, to rouse him somehow. Seeing him unconscious and helpless crushed her heart.

After the ceiling collapsed, they had to dig Gabriel out of the rubble. At first, she hadn't been sure he was alive. Blood had pooled around him and she immediately thought the worst. It would be just like life to do something so cruel as to snatch Gabriel away from her when she'd just found him again.

But he'd been alive, though badly wounded. A piece of metal scaffold had pierced his thigh. Thankfully it had missed his femoral artery but the damage was still bad. If he'd been conscious, she was certain he could've shifted into his wolf form to heal himself. But he'd yet to gain consciousness and the doctors were worried. They talked about a head injury.

Feeling tears welling in her eyes, Elise leaned forward and pressed her lips to his brow. "Wake up," she murmured into his skin.

Movement at the door caused her to sit up. A redheaded woman came into the room. She remembered her from the set when she'd first received the letter. Sophie something.

The woman nodded to her. "Sorry to interrupt."

"You didn't."

She smiled and neared the bed. "I'm Sophie. I work with Gabriel."

"Yes, I remember."

Sophie looked at Gabriel, and Elise could see the deep concern in her eyes. Lifting her hand, she reached out to touch his foot under the blanket, but hesitated then dropped it as if she'd been caught doing something she shouldn't.

Elise hadn't asked Gabriel if he'd been involved with anyone. She just assumed that he wasn't, which was probably ego on her part. But maybe there was something between him and this woman. She could understand the allure. Sophie was stunning and, by her scent, a full-blooded lycan, not a mixed blood like Elise. Not that she thought Gabriel cared about such things.

"What do the doctors say?"

"Not much. They never do tell you the total truth, do they?"

Sophie shook her head. "No, they don't."

Elise looked at Gabriel again, suddenly shaken by the sallow look in his face. She'd never worried about him like this before. She'd never seen him injured, or at least not severely. It was devastating to her. She glanced back at Sophie and wondered if she was as distressed.

"Do you think he'll wake soon?" Sophie asked Elise, as if she had all the answers.

Elise brushed the stubborn hairs from his brow again. "I don't know."

His eyes fluttered at her touch. Excited, she stroked a hand over his face again. This time his eyes came open.

"Oh, Gabriel, thank God," she murmured.

He blinked several times trying to get his bearings. Finally, his gaze settled onto Elise. Licking his lips, he tried to speak.

She quickly grabbed the water cup on the side table and set the straw at his lips. He took a few sips and nodded his thanks. His gaze then went to Sophie, who stood still at the end of the bed.

"Hey, boss," she said.

"Did you—" his voice came out dry and cracked "—find out what happened?"

She nodded. "It definitely wasn't an accident. Someone tampered with the wiring that held up the lights and ceiling panels."

He nodded. "I thought so."

Elise looked from Sophie to Gabriel. "Are you saying that accident was meant for me?"

"Yes."

She sat back in the chair, anger and remorse surging through her. Angry that someone would do this and remorseful that Gabriel had been the one injured in a trap meant for her. "I can't believe this." Elise shook her head.

Sophie took that moment to finally lay her hand on Gabriel's foot. "Are you all right, Gabe?"

"I will be. I just need to shift." He lifted his hand and touched the side of his head, where a huge black bruise had started to form along his temple and up under his hairline. "It's only a bump on the head."

Sophie smiled at him, and Elise felt she was spying on them.

But before she could stand up and give them some privacy another person bounded into the room. It was a male someone, and a vampire to boot. Grinning, he came up behind Sophie and wrapped his arms around her.

"Hey, Gabe, good to see you awake."

Sophie covered his hands with hers and she lit up like someone had turned on the light inside her body.

"We missed you," the vampire went on.

"Yeah, I bet," Gabriel said with affection.

The vampire glanced at Elise, and his eyes widened as if truly noticing her for the first time. He leaned past Sophie, without letting go of her, Elise noticed, and offered his hand. "I'm Kellen Falcon. I'm really pleased to meet you, Ms. Leroy."

She shook his hand. "Elise, please."

He nodded and went back to hugging Sophie.

Elise let out a breath she hadn't realized she was holding and, leaning forward, grabbed Gabriel's hand.

He looked down at their joined hands curiously, then up at her. "Did I miss something?"

"Just the last three hours." She gave him a half smile. "Can't a girl thank the man that saved her life?"

"It's my j—"

She put her fingers over his lips to silence him. She shook her head, tears still threatening to fall. "Don't you dare say it."

Someone, either Sophie or Kellen, cleared their throat. "We're going to go," Sophie said. "I'll come back when they're ready to release you, boss."

"I'll be out in a couple of hours."

Sophie nodded and, hand in hand with Kellen, left the hospital room.

"I think you should stay a little longer and make sure you're okay," Elise suggested. "Your leg is pretty ripped up."

Gabriel was already in the process of sitting up. "I don't need to stay. I just need to get out and shift and go for a run. I'll heal better that way."

"You're very stubborn."

"Me? I'm stubborn? Woman, you wrote the book on obstinacy."

"I'm just determined, is all."

He shook his head. "The all is, because of this, you need to shut down filming and get out of town for a bit."

"I'm not going to hide."

"Elise, this isn't some silly love letter you've received from a fan. Someone is out to harm you. If that ceiling had fallen on you…" He swallowed, as if he was having difficulty finishing his sentence. She reached for the glass cup. He closed his eyes, then continued, "You could've been killed."

She sat back in the chair and looked at him. He was all banged up and bruised, and when he moved she could see the immense pain he suffered. He had saved her life. Saved her from some deranged obsessive fan. She couldn't let his sacrifice be in vain.

Sighing, she pinched the bridge of her nose where

her pulse was thumping hard. She was going to agree to something only because it was Gabriel asking her.

"Okay. There is this lovely villa I just bought out in the country."

"Is it well-known?"

She shook her head. "Only a few people know I own it. I bought it under a different name to keep it private."

"Good. Keep it that way." He shuffled up in the bed trying to get comfortable. The blanket fell off and Elise saw his bandaged leg.

"I'm so sorry, Gabriel." The tears fell then. She couldn't stop them.

He reached across the bed and grabbed her hand. "Elise, this is not your fault. Don't take the blame for what some unstable person has done." He squeezed her hand tight. "I'm going to be fine. Nothing can keep me down for too long."

"I know," she sniffled.

"You have to promise me, though, that you're going to look after yourself. Screw what people are going to think, and stay safe."

She nodded.

But he obviously didn't believe her. "I can't do my job if I have to worry about what you're doing all the time. Promise me."

"I promise."

"Good. I'll hold you to it."

He didn't release her hand and in that moment she felt something building between them. They couldn't be in the same room together for too long without something building. But this was different, more mature.

Her gaze never leaving his, Elise stood and, leaning on the bed, she neared his mouth. When she was only a breath away, she murmured, "Gabriel, I'm still—"

"I see you're awake." A nurse charged into the room and, almost shooing Elise to the side, began to take Gabriel's stats.

Smiling wanly, Elise backed up and grabbed her purse from the chair. "I'll let you get straightened away. I'll go make arrangements."

"Okay. Good," he said. "I'll make sure the superintendent sends someone with you, so you're looked after."

"Okay." After a final awkward nod, Elise left the room. But what she really wanted to do was climb into Gabriel's bed with him and tell him exactly how much she missed him and still wanted him.

Worse, she was afraid she'd never get another chance to do so.

Chapter 10

"The mayor thinks that you're the best man for the job."

Gabriel couldn't believe what the superintendent was telling him. He'd been back at the lab for maybe a half hour before the man had cornered him in his office and sprung the bad news.

His leg was still really sore. After being released from the hospital, Gabriel had quickly driven to his favorite park, shifted and gone for a run. He couldn't run far because of his injured thigh, but just being in his wolf form had enabled him to heal a lot faster. After that, he ate red meat, then swung by the lab where he had hoped to catch up on the case.

Instead, he got sideswiped.

"You have got to be kidding me. I need to be here in the lab, doing my job. With Elise out of the city, she should be fine."

"She asked for you, Gabriel. So the decision's been made. There is no discussion."

He rubbed a hand over his face, anger welling inside. "I didn't realize I worked for Elise Leroy now."

"You don't, but you do work for me and for this city, which in turn, truthfully, is the mayor. She called him, and he called me. You know how it rolls."

"Yes, obviously."

Jakob rapped his knuckles on Gabriel's desk. "Besides, you're still injured. I would've been sending you off to recuperate anyway. So now you can recover in luxury at a beautiful country cottage."

Gabriel just looked at Jakob. What could he possibly say? It was obvious there was no room for debate or discussion. Elise had snapped her fingers and everyone had jumped.

He had wanted to truly believe she wasn't like that, that she hadn't changed into a demanding star, but some of her behavior told him otherwise. This one topped the list.

"I'll leave you to the details, Gabriel. I'm sure the case will be solved in days, a week at the most."

Gabriel nearly groaned at the prospect of spending a week with Elise in an isolated cottage. Just the two of them. He'd actually have to make conversation with her. What did he possibly have to say to her? He'd already mistakenly spilled his guts about missing her. He couldn't take that back now. It was out there. And he was sure Elise would use it to her advantage.

With an angry sigh, he picked up the phone to call his team in for a meeting. If he was going to be gone, he wanted his people to be working extra hard on the case. Every stone had to be turned, including looking into all the people who had been close to Elise over the years. Gabriel had a feeling this attack was from someone she knew and trusted. It was too close to home to be a stranger. The saboteur had gotten onto a closed set. Not an easy thing to do.

The phone on his desk rang. He picked it up. "Bellmonte."

"I heard you got hurt." It was Olena, his lead investigator.

"Nothing to worry about."

"What about the case? Do you need me? I can be back in ten hours. Cale and I are in London for a time visiting his folks."

"We're good. Don't cut your holiday short. You earned it and then some."

"Okay, but don't hesitate to call. I know how hard

it is for you to admit you need help, but don't be an ass about it."

He laughed. It was just like Olena to call it as she saw it. There was no bull crap with her. "I will."

"Uh-uh. We'll see." And with that she hung up. That's what he liked about Olena—she was no-nonsense. He figured she'd be the one who took his job eventually.

Forty minutes later, most of his team had assembled in his office. Sophie, Kellen, Francois and the other head investigator, Maria Serrano, sat around his office as he laid it out.

"I've been recruited to be Ms. Leroy's bodyguard while she's out of town so it's up to you guys to put this case together and quickly."

Kellen smiled. "So, the two of you are going to shack up together somewhere all quiet and private like?"

Gabriel glared at Sophie. The lycan decidedly couldn't keep her mouth shut.

She shrugged under his scrutiny. "*Que?* I couldn't help it. That's just too much to keep to myself. I mean, you, Gabriel Bellmonte, had a relationship with the most beautiful and talented actress in the world. It's too odd and strange to not tell everyone."

Everyone nodded in agreement.

He ignored it. "Can we talk about the case, please?"

Everyone nodded in agreement again.

"Where are we with the prints?"

Maria noted from the report she was holding. "We ran the extra set of prints on the letter through our database. We got a hit. They belong to Reginald Alcott."

"The director?" Sophie asked.

Maria nodded. "Looks like he was arrested in 1886 for participating in the Haymarket Massacre in Chicago where eight police officers were killed by a bomb. There was no real evidence against him so he was released."

"I remember that day," Kellen said. "I wasn't in Chicago but I do remember it."

Gabriel ran a hand through his unruly hair. "Wow, I didn't know we had records from that long ago."

"You'd be surprised what we have on file," Maria said.

"Okay, obviously Elise's assistant was mistaken on who touched the letter. She must've called him to come look at it and forgot that she'd done that."

"Or he is the culprit," Francois added.

Gabriel shook his head. "No, I'm pretty sure it's not him. But to be on the safe side, we need to have a long talk with him. And with Lily, Elise's assistant. There's something going on there with her, I'm sure of it. She's keeping something secret. It might have nothing to do with what is going on with Elise, but we need to be sure."

Maria flipped open her cell phone. "I'll make the call."

While she barked orders into her phone, Gabriel looked at Sophie. "Any leads on the sabotage?"

She glanced at Kellen. "I checked at the way it was rigged and there's nothing there of too much interest. The wires had been frayed. The perp could've used just about any instrument for that. No marks to indicate any specific tool that we could track. It did look like a rush job, though, so that might be something. Maybe he or she was interrupted. Or they only had a small window of opportunity."

Gabriel nodded. "That's good info, actually. Check with the front gate guard and get a list of everyone who was in and out the night before or the very early morning."

Sophie jotted down notes in her notebook, a habit she'd picked up from Gabriel. "Will do."

"Anything from the charity event? Any leads there?"

She shook her head. "We have no witnesses. The vehicle was scratched with either a knife or a sharp piece of metal. Not much to follow there."

"Any word on the driver?"

"No. He's still missing," Sophie said.

"Let's get a warrant to check his place. I don't think he's involved, but we need to make sure."

She wrote that down. "Okay, boss."

Maria ended her call and flipped her phone closed. "The director is on his way here to make a statement. I couldn't get a hold of the assistant."

Gabriel sighed. "I can talk to her when I go to Elise's to pick her up."

Kellen chuckled. "So, where are you two going? Romantic hideaway?"

Gabriel gave the vampire a hard stare. "Do you like your job here, Falcon?"

Kellen shrugged playfully. "It's okay, I guess. A raise would rock, though, if you're offering."

"I'm not. And you're lucky you have a job. If Sophie wasn't so enamored with you, I would've shipped you back to Necropolis."

Kellen jumped to his feet, Sophie along with him. "Oh, I know you like me, Gabe, so don't play coy."

Gabriel shook his head, but appreciated the vampire's humor. Despite his theatrics and the loud hardcore music he played in his lab, he liked Kellen. He'd been a good addition to his team.

"I'll keep you apprised of our status, Gabriel," Maria said. She offered him her hand. He took it and shook it, appreciating her thoughtfulness. "Have a safe trip."

"Thanks, Maria."

She left. Francois followed her out without many words. The young witch had lost some of his vigor when Olena had married the Interpol agent who had worked on a case with them last year. Francois had been in love with her for a long time. That left Sophie and Kellen to aggravate him.

"I'll call you if anything happens," Sophie said.

"Call me even if nothing happens. I hate being out of contact."

"You just don't want to be alone with Ms. Leroy," Kellen needled him.

Gabriel stood and was about to come around the desk when Sophie pushed on Kellen's chest to take him out of the room. "We're going, Gabe. Stay safe."

"Yeah, remember to use a condom," Kellen said just as he was dragged out of the door.

Gabriel was angry, but not at Kellen. He enjoyed the vampire's good-natured ribbing. He didn't often get that, as he didn't have many male friends. Certainly not anyone he would confide in, or confess that he still had feelings for Elise and wasn't sure if he was strong enough to be around her for a few days without acting on those emotions. There was no one from his pack that he felt close to. One of his closer lycan pack members had died last year in the bombing of a nightclub. Coincidentally, Kellen had been the one who had tried to save him. The vampire had saved Sophie and hundreds more, as well.

He wished someone would save him right about now, because he had a feeling he was heading for one giant disaster.

Chapter 11

Gabriel pressed the button on the intercom at the gate to Elise's home and spoke into the built-in microphone. "Inspector Gabriel Bellmonte."

"ID, please," the male guard said.

Gabriel slid out his wallet, opened it to his badge and put it up to the small camera. After a few seconds, the gate started to open.

He drove the rented Mercedes through the gate and parked in the loop at the front door. He figured Elise would appreciate a luxury car instead of the older sedan he used for work. The door opened before he even got out of the vehicle. Lily stood there waiting for him. She smiled when he approached.

"Elise will be ready in a moment."

Gabriel followed her into the house. She led him to the main sitting room. "Would you like something to drink?"

He shook his head. "No, but I would like to ask you a few more questions, if that would be okay?"

She eyed him sidelong. "I guess, if you think it would help Elise's case."

"I understand Inspector Serrano called you."

"Hmm, I don't think so."

"She said she left a message for you to call her."

She shrugged. "I didn't get a message."

"There were four sets of prints on the letter, Lily. Why didn't you tell me that Reginald Alcott also touched it before we arrived?"

"I guess I forgot." She folded her hands in front of her. He wondered if it was to stop the little shake he saw in them. "There was a lot of stuff going on at the time—it's easy to forget some details."

"That's true." He was glad to have his suspicions confirmed. He didn't think the director was their letter writer. "Is there anything else you are forgetting to divulge?"

"No." Her voice went up an octave. He heard the slight infliction in its timbre. She was definitely hiding something.

"I know there's something, Lily. You may not think it has anything to do with Elise's situation, but you could be wrong. I know how much you care for her, and I know you wouldn't want to be keeping the one piece of information that could break this case."

Angry now, her cheeks flared pink. "I resent the implication that I would ever do anything to harm Elise. I have been nothing but cooperative with you and have answered all your damn questions. I have nothing further to say to you."

But before she could escape from the sitting room, Elise filled the doorway. "It's okay, Lily, you can tell him."

Lily stopped in her tracks, frowning. "Excuse me? I don't have anything to tell."

Elise moved farther into the room, her gaze on Lily. Gabriel could see a sorrow in her eyes. "It's all right, Lily. I know. You don't have to keep it secret any longer."

Tears started to trickle down Lily's cheeks. "Elise, please, I don't know what you're talking about."

When Elise reached the witch, she placed her hand on her wet cheek. "I know about you and Diego, Lily. I've known for some time now."

Lily's head dipped and the tears fell unhindered, dotting the ivory rug at her feet. "I'm so sorry," she sobbed. Elise gathered the girl in her arms and hugged her close. She patted her back and made small soothing noises to her.

Gabriel felt extremely uncomfortable watching this unfold. He knew Lily had been hiding something, but he hadn't thought an affair with Diego Martinez was what she was holding back. He hadn't even considered it. And he wasn't sure if the affair had anything to do with Elise's case or not. He was at a loss for words.

"Um, maybe I should wait in the car."

Elise looked at him over Lily's shoulder and shook her head. She pulled back and rubbed her thumbs over Lily's cheeks brushing away the tears. "It's all right, *ma belle.*"

"You're not going to fire me?" she stuttered.

"Of course not. I could never replace you."

Lily chewed on her bottom lip. "I'm so sorry, Elise. I don't know how it happened. It just did, then I got caught up in it and it just steamrolled from there."

"I understand. Diego has his charms, however hidden they may be."

Lily wiped at her eyes. "I'll break it off, I swear I will. You're more important to me than he is."

"I know." Elise pressed a kiss to her forehead.

Still wiping at her red-rimmed eyes, Lily turned and looked at Gabriel. "Bet this wasn't what you were expecting to hear."

"No, not really," he said, "but it would explain

where you were the night Elise's car was vandalized. You were with Diego, yes?"

She nodded. "Doing it in the cloakroom of all places. I can't even believe how tacky that is. His date was off dancing with someone else at the time."

"Yes, but it does provide Diego with an alibi."

Elise turned her gaze toward him. "I didn't realize that Diego was even a suspect."

"Everyone's a suspect at this point. Everyone who knows you or has had a close relationship with you at sometime or another. The perp knows your habits and your schedule. Not just any stranger off the street can get access to that information."

Lily eyed him curiously, her cheeks still streaked with tears. "I'm not a suspect, am I?"

Elise chuckled. "Of course, you're not." But her smile fell when Gabriel didn't quickly agree. "You can't be serious, Gabriel."

"Everyone is a suspect until they're not."

Elise shook her head. "Well, that's just ridiculous." She patted Lily on the shoulder.

"I get to decide what's ridiculous, this time around."

Pursing her lips, she eyed him carefully then she turned and smiled at Lily. "Could you grab my bags for me? And bring them to the front door?"

Lily nodded and, after wiping at her face one last

time, walked out of the living room to do as Elise asked.

Twirling a ring on her finger, Elise walked toward him. "Are we really back there, again, Gabriel?"

"What?"

"You know what. Fifteen years ago."

Gabriel moved away from her and started for the front door. "We should hit the road if we want to make it to your cottage before dark."

But she wouldn't let him escape. She moved with him, matching him step for step. Finally, she caught him, or he let her catch him, he wasn't sure which. Standing in front of him, she laid her hand against his cheek. "It's not your fault, Gabriel. What happened to me all those years ago was an accident. You couldn't have changed it."

"I could have, if you had let me." There was pain in his chest. It felt tight and he found it hard to breathe. He wanted to wrap her in his arms, to press his lips to hers and taste her again. But he beat the urge down like forcing a wild beast back into its cage.

"It's not your job to save everyone."

"It is now." He lifted his hand and trailed his fingers along her shoulder down to the dip in her blouse. There he found the scar just above her right breast. It was small, nearly invisible now, but he saw it. He knew it was there.

It was where his best friend, Yves Martin, had torn at Elise's flesh over fifteen years ago. It was Gabriel's scar as much as it was hers. It was a reminder to Gabriel that he'd failed in the most important test of his life—keeping the love of his life safe.

She covered his hand with her own. "You didn't know Yves was rabid, Gabriel. You couldn't have known that he would attack me."

"If I hadn't been late that night meeting you…"

She shook her head. "It's not your fault. You saved my life, remember? You were the one who pulled him off me. You healed me."

"If only you hadn't been so reckless and had done what I asked of you."

She squeezed his hand then. "What? I wasn't reckless."

"You were always reckless. And I don't think things have changed much."

She dropped her hand from his and moved away. He squeezed his hand into a fist; his fingers still tingled from where he'd touched her.

"Why can't you let go of this, Gabriel? Forgive yourself, move on. I have."

"Yeah, I've noticed." He shoved his hands into his jacket pockets although what he wanted to do was fill his hands with her again. "I'll be outside, at the car. Don't take too long."

Without waiting for her response, Gabriel brushed

past her and left the room. He marched down the hall and out the front door. Only when he stepped outside did he allow himself to expel the breath he'd been holding. Taking in a few gulps of air, he went to the car and leaned against it for support.

He was a fool. He'd angered her only because of the deep-seated guilt that he couldn't let go. He hated himself for upsetting her, especially about that night. But to do any less he would've broken down. He would've dropped to his knees and begged her to forgive him. Begged her to love him again. He hadn't realized how much she truly meant to him, would always mean to him, until he'd sensed she was in trouble. Right before he pushed her out of the way, Gabriel knew he still loved Elise. And would until the day he died.

Chapter 12

The two-hour drive to Elise's country cottage was a long, agonizing test of patience. Thank technology for the blessed triumph of the iPhone. While Gabriel drove, Elise checked email, read a few magazines electronically and caught up on the latest industry gossip.

She hadn't had time to do any of that lately, so she appreciated the moments she got to indulge, even if it was spent in a vehicle with a brooding sangloup who refused to speak more than four sentences to her. *"Do you need to use the facilities?"* was at the top of that list.

The moment Gabriel turned into the dirt lane

leading up to her cottage, Elise felt better, as if a huge load of rocks had been lifted from her shoulders. Smiling, she gazed out the window as he rolled the car up the tree-lined driveway to the house. When the quaint cottage came into view, she sighed happily.

She'd recently bought the place, and had only spent a week here, but that week had been heavenly. She'd puttered around the house, tended the garden and gone for many long runs through the neighboring forest. It had been the most relaxed she'd been in years. And now she was back in hopes of finding that same sense of peace.

Glancing at Gabriel, she didn't think that was going to be quite as achievable as before.

Once the car was stopped, she pushed open her door and stepped out. Taking in a deep breath of crisp clean air, she said, "Now, isn't this a piece of heaven?"

Gabriel was out of the car and looking around. He nodded. "It's nice."

Nice? Leave it to Gabriel to make the biggest understatement of the year. "It's more than nice. It's absolutely a picture of perfection."

He was busy at the back of the vehicle, taking out her bags—she'd brought three—and his measly pack. He shut the trunk and, carrying all the bags, he started for the front door. He pushed open the wooden gate that fenced in the front lawn and flower garden with his foot. "Reminds me of Bebe's place."

Elise halted on the stone path to the house and put her hand on her hip, really looking at the cottage. Bebe had been her grandmother. She and Gabriel had spent a lot of time together at her small cottage just outside the commune of Rodez, in the south of France, where both she and Gabriel grew up.

Because of their families' feuding, they didn't get many chances to be alone together. Bebe had offered them a sanctuary to explore their blossoming love. She'd never bought into the fight between the Leroys and the Bellmontes. She'd thought it a load of old-world bunk. She'd been right, of course. Bebe had been right about a lot of things.

Elise still missed her. Especially on days like these. She'd been dead going on ten years now, but Elise could still remember the scent on her skin and the delectable smells of home-baked biscuits cooling on the windowsill freshly made for her and Gabriel's weekly visits.

Shaking off the maudlin feeling from the memories, Elise stepped through the open front door and into the main living room of the cottage. The light through the floor-to-ceiling windows flooded the room, making her smile. That was one of the features that had made her buy the place—the glorious light in all parts of the house. Shadows found it hard to hide in her cottage.

"Where do your bags go?" Gabriel asked from the huge country kitchen that the living room opened up into.

"This way." She motioned toward the hallway off the kitchen. She walked down it, Gabriel following her to the two bedrooms that dominated the other half of the cottage.

She walked into the main bedroom, which never failed to put a little skip in her belly. She loved this room. It was open and airy and had its own patio, which curved around the backyard and garden. She stepped to the double glass doors and threw them open, taking in a deep gulp of floral-scented air.

She turned around just as Gabriel set her bags down near the big canopied bed. "Your room is next door. It has its own bathroom, as well."

He nodded and then disappeared into the next room. Elise turned back to the open glass doors and stepped out onto the wooden patio. She glanced at the well-stocked garden and flexed her hands. She was itching to get in there and reap the rewards. She had her grounds tended to while she was gone, but this morning she had Lily call the people and tell them that their services were not needed this week. Elise planned to do the work herself.

Turning, she walked back into the bedroom,

through it and peered around the corner into the other room. Gabriel was standing at the huge window staring out into the surrounding woods. He turned to meet her gaze.

There was an odd look on his face. One of longing, she supposed. She wondered how long it had been since he'd been out of the city and able to run through the trees unhindered by anything other than the brambles catching at his fur.

"We can go for a run tonight, if you like. There's a stream not far from here. The water's a bit cool but on a warm summer evening, it's refreshing."

He half smiled. "Sounds good. I can't remember the last time I went for a country run."

"Well, it's time you did. I'm going to put my things away, then I think we should pop into the village and grab some groceries. We don't need vegetables. I can get them from the garden, but some meat and fresh bread. We can eat out on the patio."

"You can cook?" he asked, just a hint of humor in his voice.

She snorted. "Of course I can. Bebe taught me everything she knew before she passed on."

"Well, then it should be a great meal."

"You bet it will be." She bounced around on the balls of her feet, feeling lighter and freer than she had in years. "I won't be long. I'll meet you in the living room when I'm done."

Without waiting she returned to her room and tossed her first bag onto the bed to unpack. She unzipped it and drew out a pair of shorts. It was the perfect thing to wear on such a beautiful day. She could almost forget about the awful things that had happened in the past few days. It was as if it had never happened and she was here on a holiday to rest her mind, body and soul.

But she heard Gabriel moving around in the next room and knew that he wasn't here on a vacation. He was only here with her to keep an eye on her, to protect her from someone who wanted to harm her. Her little fantasy vaporized in a moment, and she walked over to the large four-tier dresser, opened one of the drawers and shoved her shorts into them.

Maybe tomorrow would be a better day to wear them.

Chapter 13

After putting things away in their respective rooms, the two of them drove into the village near the cottage and stopped at the only store that had groceries.

It was a quaint little shop that sold homemade jams, candles and other goodies. There was a homey apple-pie smell in the place and Gabriel admitted he'd taken in a few greedy gulps of it. It reminded him of the small town he'd been raised in.

And he found when he watched her now, strolling through the aisles of the shop setting various things into the basket she carried on her arm, he could still see the wide-eyed innocent child she'd been. So full of life and questions and wonder about the world.

She was only a few years younger than him, but when she was a child, sometimes she seemed so much younger. He'd always felt protective of her. Even before he developed romantic feelings for her as she'd blossomed into a beautiful woman.

She smiled at him over the shelf with the little figurines made out of river rocks. He returned her smile, the first sense of relaxation starting to settle in. He rolled his shoulders and tried to let it fill him completely. It would be nice to lighten up for a little bit. He couldn't remember the last time he'd had a holiday.

Elise bought some meat, including a couple of thick, juicy T-bone steaks, a loaf of whole-grain bread baked that day, fruit, and a few tasty pastries. Not many people knew he had a sweet tooth, but Elise did. After he thanked her for the pastries, they put the things in the back of the vehicle.

"Could we walk for a bit before we head back?" Elise gestured to the old-fashioned cobblestone street that ran down the middle of the hamlet.

"Sure."

They strolled down the street together, near each other but not quite touching. Every store window they passed, Elise had to look in. When she saw something she liked, she'd point to it. He didn't comment, just nodded his head.

The hamlet was nice, the street quiet. The few

people who passed them on the sidewalk would smile and say *"Bonjour,"* as they walked on by. No one stopped to stare at Elise or ask for her autograph or take a picture. She must've been in her glory just being a regular person, doing a regular thing like window-shopping with a friend.

"It's beautiful here," she said.

He nodded. "Yeah, it's peaceful. I imagine not much happens here."

She smiled. "Hmm, wouldn't that be great. To live in a place where not much happens." She laughed.

He laughed, too. "Sure would."

"I think we've both had enough of stuff happening to fill ten lifetimes."

"I reckon so."

She wrapped her hands around his arm. His first instinct would've been to pull away, but he didn't. He liked that she touched him. He liked strolling down the street with her, with nowhere to go, nothing to do. And no one bothering them.

"When I retire, this is where I'm going to live."

He glanced at her, a bit surprised. "Are you thinking of retiring from acting?"

She nodded. "I think about it all the time. More in the past couple of years. I'm tired, Gabriel. I want to do something else now with my life."

"I thought you enjoyed it."

"I do. I love it. My muse loves it. But it's time to

move on. I want something else in my life now. I want the things that I've been missing." She looked at him. "Don't you?"

He didn't answer, but it was in his mind the whole time they walked back to the vehicle and returned to the cottage. He did want the things he'd been missing. A house, a yard, a woman he could love for the rest of his days. Over the years, these things had crossed his mind, but never more so than in the past few days.

Gabriel watched from the kitchen patio as Elise tilled in the garden. After retuning to the cottage, they'd put the groceries away and Elise had changed her clothes and wandered out into the yard. She was pulling up the carrots and onions that she was planning to cook for dinner.

He liked watching her, especially when she didn't know it. She was so insanely lovely, it was impossible to keep his eyes off her. She was like a golden angel floating around on the ground. Her every movement seemed effortless. All of those things about her made her into the star she was.

And into the woman he'd always longed for.

Carrying the vegetables into the house, Elise passed him on the patio. "I'm going to make the salad while you fire up the grill." She nodded toward the long stainless-steel grill situated at the end of the patio.

Resigned, he moved toward the piece of equipment and started it up. He guessed it wouldn't hurt anything if he played along. They were in the beautiful countryside and it was a gorgeous evening. He wouldn't be neglecting his job if he relaxed a little and enjoyed the evening. He was hungry and he was curious to taste Elise's cooking.

An hour later, they were sitting out on the deck eating. Gabriel had grilled the steaks and Elise had made the rest. And he had to admit he couldn't remember the last time he'd enjoyed a meal more.

They'd talked about old times, but not about their relationship, just about mutual friends and their respective family members. It was nice to catch up on Elise's family. He remembered her mother. She'd been nice to him and kind. Elise also had a younger sister, Yvette, whom he'd liked. Elise told him Yvette had moved to Spain and was a painter. She'd married and had children. Elise had two nephews whom she adored.

"What about your parents? Are they still in the same old house?"

He nodded. "I get letters from my mother. She's well."

"And your father?"

"He died a few years back."

"Oh, I'm sorry." She reached across the table and gripped his hand. "I didn't know."

"It's all right. We never did get along. He'd always been a bastard. My brother, Antoine, plans to take over the land and house."

"He married?"

She pulled her hand away, and he was intensely aware of the loss of heat over his skin.

"Yeah, a lycan. They have four children already. Two sets of twins."

Elise's eyes went wide and she laughed. "Wow, I can't imagine little Antoine married with four babies to look after."

He laughed, too. "I know. It's a miracle to me that the oldest are already five."

"Do you see them often?"

He shook his head. "Not often enough."

She rested her head on her hand and regarded him curiously. "I can picture you with them. Uncle Gabriel. You probably spoil them rotten."

"Maybe." But he smiled. He did spoil his nephews and nieces. He brought them sweets and presents every time he visited.

She dropped her hand and placed it in her lap. She fidgeted with her napkin. "And you? You never came close to getting married and having your own children?"

He kept her gaze for a moment, seeing the emotion in the dark green. The attack on Elise had rendered her infertile. She could never give birth to children. He'd always wondered if she thought that had been one of the reasons he'd left.

"No. Never even close."

She gave him a half smile then stood. She started to gather the plates from the table. "I'll toss these in the sink. Then we can go for that run. I think we both need one."

Gabriel stood and helped her carry the dirty dishes into the kitchen. When that was done, they walked out through the patio doors, across the lawn and into the woods without any words. They didn't need any. Not now.

Once they were just inside the copse of trees, Gabriel started to undress. He took off his shirt, folded it and set it on the ground, then shed his pants, folding those, as well.

"I see you still fold your clothes."

He turned to look at Elise. She was breathtakingly naked and her clothes were strewn about as if she'd tossed them here and there. Which she most likely had. It was hard to look at her without desire. He wanted her—he couldn't deny that—and fighting it was proving to be more difficult by the second.

He averted his gaze. "An old habit," he said as he pulled down his boxers and folded them on top of his pants.

When he was completely naked, he fell to all fours to transform. Elise did the same. And as their gazes met, they both started the shift.

It was a painful thing to shift. Bones snapped and elongated and changed. Skin pulled and twisted. Coarse hair popped through too-small skin pores. The jaw and head were always the worst. Sometimes it felt like railway spikes were being pounded into the skull, and teeth were being pulled with a set of pliers.

But thankfully it was quick.

Five minutes later they were both in their wolf forms. Gabriel stretched out his legs, all four of them, and snorted through his nostrils. Then he lifted his head and inhaled the new scents that permeated the clean, crisp air. Mosses and leaves and mold, and the fresh trail of a chipmunk. But it was *her* scent that filled him to bursting.

He turned to look for her, but she was already on the move. She glanced over at him and huffed two times then continued through the trees. She wanted him to chase her. It was a game they'd played before. As a wolf, he was always up for games, reveled in them. It was as a man that he didn't allow himself to indulge.

So the chase was on.

They ran through the woods, jumping over fallen logs and zigzagging through thick underbrush. Periodically, Gabriel overtook her, but then moments later he would fall back and let her take the lead. Back and forth they went like that until they reached the shallow stream in the small clearing. It was then that Gabriel made his move.

As Elise bent down to lap at the water, he leaped toward her. Swiping at her body, he took her down and they both went tumbling sideways into the cool water. She yelped as they went under and tried to turn to nip at his hind legs. But he held her down by the sheer force of his weight.

She struggled beneath him, and then finally got her jaws around his muzzle. She bit down and it hurt. Gabriel got the message and jumped up, releasing his hold on her. He guessed the game was over.

After a good shake to get the water off, Elise bounded back into the trees. Gabriel followed her, giving her room but also keeping an eye on her. Even as a wolf, maybe more so, his protective nature took over. He'd never let anything harm Elise. If any other animal, human or otherwise, threatened her in any way, he'd attack. Without a second thought.

Whether it was official or not, and no matter what had happened to them in the past or would happen to them in the future, Elise belonged to him. He'd claimed her many years ago. And just because time had passed didn't make it less so.

Elise made it to the edge of the wood where they

had left their clothing. Huffing once then twice, as was her way, she crouched down preparing to shift back to human.

That was when Gabriel caught a new scent. A scent that hadn't been there before. It was strong and offensive to his nose.

It was the strong, spiced smell of vampire.

Elise was halfway through her shift when Gabriel bounded down the tree line following the scent trail. It ran along the woods within watching distance of the villa. He chased it, hoping to come across its owner, all the way to the road. It ended there. Whoever it belonged to had a vehicle waiting.

Gabriel ran back and forth along the ditch hoping to catch more scents, but there wasn't anything else left. Nothing as strong or as recent. Glancing down the road to see if he could spot a car, he stepped out onto the cement. There was nothing, though, in either direction.

Satisfied he'd done what he could, he returned to the edge of the wood. Elise was there, in human form, sitting in the grass waiting for him, her long hair still damp. Once he returned, he crouched down, closed his eyes and forced the shift upon his body.

It was just as painful coming back as going forward. Once it was done, he rested on his back for a bit.

"What did you smell?" she asked.

"Vampire."

"Recent?"

He nodded. "I followed it to the road. Whoever it was, was watching the house from the woods then ran back to their car once we returned." He sat up and ran a hand through his wet hair.

"Paparazzi, maybe?"

"Maybe." Standing, he retrieved his clothing and put it on. When he was done, Elise was standing waiting for him.

They walked back to the villa, the magic of their reunion run through the woods gone with the knowledge that maybe they'd been found.

Chapter 14

For the twentieth time, Elise flipped over onto her back and stared at the ceiling above her bed. A predawn glow filtered through the windows. It was not yet five and she couldn't get comfortable enough to close her eyes and drift away.

Sleep had been hard to come by. After they returned to the villa, each preoccupied with their own thoughts, Elise found it next to impossible to recover what little balance in their relationship they had found in the woods. It had been destroyed by Gabriel's discovery of someone's presence at the villa.

Elise wasn't naive enough to consider that it had been some harmless neighbor out and about. She had no close neighbors, for one thing, and the villa was surrounded by trees for another. No vampire was going traipsing through the trees for fun. A lycan possibly, but not a vampire. There was one road in and out of the property. If someone traveled it, it was because they were looking for her or had gotten lost. She was betting on the former.

Flinging the blankets aside, she sat up and swung her legs over the side of the bed to touch the floor. Thankfully she had a rug in her room, because she had a feeling it would've been cold on her feet otherwise. There was a slight chill in the air. She stood, grabbed the robe that had been folded over the dressing chair and slid it on. She found a pair of slippers, put them on, and then left her room.

In the hallway, she paused at Gabriel's closed door. She put a hand to the wood, wanting desperately to open the door and go to him. Instead she pressed her ear to the door and listened for him inside. She couldn't hear anything, not even the slow intakes of air indicating he was asleep.

She pushed away from the door and continued down the hall to the kitchen. She'd make tea and then take it out to the patio and watch the sunrise. Maybe it would lift her heart a little.

As she reached to open the cupboard door, something in her peripheral vision caught her attention.

Leaving the cupboard door open, she crossed the kitchen and opened the sliding patio door.

Gabriel swung around in the chair he'd been slumped in. A coffee cup sat at the side of the chair on the patio.

"What are you doing here?" she asked, although by the wrung-out look of him she suspected he'd been sitting on the patio all night, or at least most of it.

"Couldn't sleep," he said, yawning and then stretching his arms.

"You've been out here all night." She padded across the patio and stood at the edge to stare beyond the yard, to the edge of the woods.

"Not all night."

She turned to look at him. "Well, now that I'm awake, I'll make you breakfast, then you can get some sleep."

Without another word, she turned around, intending to go back into the kitchen. But Gabriel grabbed her arm before she could pass him.

She looked down at him and opened her mouth to say something, but closed it when she saw the look in his eyes. The look of years of yearning.

She let him pull her closer. And when he wrapped his arms around her waist and buried his head into her stomach, she gently hugged his head close, stroking his hair with her hands. She closed her eyes and drew him in. It had been too long since she'd held him like this. Too long since she'd felt the heat of his body next to hers. And now that she had him in her arms she had no intention of letting him go even if he pulled away. There was no retreat this time around. They would finish it here and now.

"Elise, I—"

"Hush. No words, Gabriel. We don't need them. Not today."

She drew him up into a stand, then wrapped her arms around him and kissed him. Burying his hands into her hair, he pulled her closer and deepened the kiss.

It was hot and hard and full of so many things, past and present, that it made her head spin. She dug her fingers into his back for balance.

His lips still on hers, Gabriel reached down and swept her up into his arms. He carried her, pressing his lips to her chin and neck, across the patio. He slid open the door with his foot, then strode across the kitchen down the hall to her bedroom.

In three long strides he was across the room and kneeling on the bed to lay her down on it. When she was settled, he pulled back and, standing near the edge of the bed, removed his clothes. She watched every movement he made, reveling in every inch of skin revealed. Gabriel was a beautiful man powerfully built, with long, lean muscles that bunched and pulled as he took off his shirt, then his pants.

When he returned to kneel on the mattress, he was naked and she drank her fill of him. She'd seen him naked before, years ago, and just yesterday, but this was different. Removing one's clothing to shift wasn't a sexual act. A sensual one most definitely, as her lycan side was definitely in tune with all her primal needs. But seeing him, here, now, his sublime body poised above her, ready and willing to share himself with her, sent a rush of pleasurable shivers down her back. She wanted to feel that hard flesh of his on hers. No, she *needed* to, just as much as she needed to take her next breath of air.

Lying beside her, he untied her robe and pushed back both sides. She sat up and allowed him to pull the satin from her body. Thankfully, she slept in the nude so there were no more barriers between them.

Slowly, he traced his fingers over her body. Starting at her collarbone, he trailed his hands down over her breasts. He cupped one and rubbed his thumb over her hard, throbbing nipple. She gasped a little as he bent down and took it into his mouth, brushing his tongue over her again and again.

She'd had lovers before, but none whom she'd wanted as much as Gabriel. Fifteen years had not diminished her desire for him. But they had both grown, both matured, both experienced so much in their lives, that lovemaking now would be so much more. She knew it in her very bones that making love to Gabriel would destroy any possible future with others. After this, she'd not want another man. Ever. She'd never be truly happy without Gabriel ever again.

But she was ready for that. From the moment she laid eyes on him again in her trailer, she knew this moment would come. Fifteen years ago, she was his and that hadn't changed. Despite all that had transpired between them and within their separate lives, they were mated. Nothing could break that bond.

After lavishing attention on both her breasts, Gabriel poised himself above her body, his arms shaking with barely controlled restraint. All she could feel was the heat of him and it radiated between her legs. Spreading them, she hooked her heels onto his hips and brought him down to meet her.

Gabriel nestled his cock against the soft folds of her sex. She was already wet and open, and he pressed into her with ease. Elise raked her nails over his skin when he filled her completely, everything inside her stretching to accommodate him.

As he slid back and forth, she moaned into his ear. He felt incredible inside her, filling her emptiness. Emptiness she hadn't realized existed until now.

Gabriel licked the side of her neck, moving his mouth over her flesh. He nibbled on her chin and found her eager mouth with his own. Bringing his hands up, he buried them in her hair while they kissed.

Every nerve in her body responded to him. To his touch, to his taste. She moaned into his mouth and nipped hungrily at his lips. She wanted to devour him. Raw animal need consumed her. Something she hadn't felt in so long. With Gabriel, it went beyond the physical longing. Deep inside her psyche and her soul, she yearned for him. She'd forgotten what it was like to need so fiercely.

Elise wrapped her arms around him and rolled him over onto his back. "I've missed you. I've missed this." Gabriel stared into her eyes as she straddled him, his long length still deep inside her.

She started to rock on him, slow at first then gaining her rhythm. As flickers of pleasure surged up her body, she started to pump faster, harder. Slamming herself down onto him, losing herself to him. The sounds of flesh against flesh reverberated around them in the room.

Gabriel reached up and molded her breasts in his hands, flicking his thumbs over her peaked nipples. He trailed a hand down her torso, caressing her skin to where they joined. His fingers found her wet cleft, cleverly nudging his knuckle against her most sensitive spot.

Jolts of fire rang up her body. She could feel her

orgasm tightening deep inside her belly. It would not take much more to push her, drive her, over the edge and into bliss.

Gabriel gripped a hand around her waist and stilled her motions. "Not so fast. I want to feel every inch of you. I've waited so long to have you again."

With both hands, he encircled her hips, slowing her movement. He lifted her up slowly along his cock, held her still with just the tip of him inside, and then brought her down inch by excruciating inch until he filled her entirely again. He did this several times.

Elise could barely contain herself. All her muscles and nerve endings began to hum and vibrate. His slow, exquisite torture was sending her spiraling to the edge, hovering in midair. Her sex contracted around him as her climax slammed into her with an explosive force.

Crying out, she fell forward to bury her face into the warmth on his neck. He wrapped his arms around her and continued to stroke inside her, and his orgasm came soon after. She could feel every surge of his seed inside her.

Clamping her eyes shut against the tears that welled there, she felt like a dam burst inside her. Emotions long ago dried up came rushing to the surface. She took in a ragged breath, finding it difficult to contain them.

Gabriel kissed the side of her neck as his orgasm subsided. She could feel his hot breath on her sensitive skin. By the intake of breath, she could tell he wanted to say something, but instead he resigned himself to kissing her on the cheek and resting his head against hers.

The tears leaked out despite her closed eyes. So she opened them, and watched as Gabriel licked them away from her cheeks. She gave him a half smile, words still locked deep inside her, then rested her head on his chest.

He wrapped his arms around her, stroking his hands up and down her back. And there they lay until the sun peeked over the horizon and bathed the day in a bright yellow hue.

Chapter 15

For the rest of the day, Gabriel and Elise fell into a comfortable routine with each other. Their lovemaking had cut a certain edge off their interaction and they were both able to relax a little.

After a hearty breakfast that they prepared together, they set out to tend to the garden. Gabriel pulled the weeds while Elise reaped the rest of the vegetables that they would use for their meals to come.

Gabriel enjoyed the menial task of digging out the weeds from the dirt. He hadn't used his hands for more than collecting evidence and writing reports in a long time. When he was a boy, he loved nothing more than to till the land and plant seeds to watch them grow. He was a farmer's son through and through. But his other needs, his other hopes and desires, had pushed him toward a life in law enforcement when he grew up. He was never sure his dad ever understood his ambition to be a crime-scene analyst.

He supposed it never really mattered though, as his father and he never got along, never saw eye to eye in any matter. And that was especially true when it came to Elise.

His father had forbidden him to see her, to form a relationship with her. The feud between their families was very much ingrained in his father. As it had been instilled in him from his father before him. And so on, all the way back four hundred years earlier to the first Bellmonte and first Leroy, one a lycan and one a vampire, who had once been the best of friends but had fallen out over a woman and a chunk of land.

Lifting his gaze from his work, Gabriel watched Elise as she dug up potatoes. She was barefoot, ankle deep in the soil and, by the radiant smile on her face, loving every minute of it. Sometimes it took his breath away to look at her. She was crazy beautiful, but it was more than that. She had a light inside her. Something that glowed when she was truly happy. And it was glowing bright right now.

It filled him with joy to see her like that. And to know he had turned the light back on inside her.

But he wasn't sure how long he could fuel it for. After the case, he was unsure how to proceed. He wasn't convinced they could truly be together. He had never been certain of their relationship. He wanted her—that was no lie, and impossible to fight any longer—and he knew she wanted him as well, but he wasn't sure it was enough. Love sometimes just wasn't sufficient to survive the heartaches and heartbreaks.

He stood, wiped his dirty hands onto his increasingly soiled jeans and stretched out his back. It was a good stretch, one birthed from good hard labor. He walked over to where Elise still dug in the ground and bent down to collect the potatoes she'd unearthed.

"Looks like potatoes au gratin, tonight," he said.

"Oh, really? And are you cooking it?" She put one elegant hand, streaked with dirt, on her hip and cocked her one eyebrow. It was a stance he'd often seen her take. It was flirty and sexy and one-hundred-percent Elise Leroy.

"Maybe I can be persuaded."

With a spark in her eye, she dropped the spade and literally pounced on him. As he caught her around the waist, he brought her mouth against his. The kiss was hot and hard and furious. He could taste the earth and the sun and the sweat from her body. Tastes he savored as he sampled her mouth with his lips, tongue and teeth.

As he kissed her, she wrapped herself around him and he carried her over to the water tap and hose. He set her down and pulled away from her. Smiling, he bent down to grab the hose.

Hers eyes widened. "You wouldn't."

"Wouldn't I?" With a quick twist of his wrist he turned the tap and cold water burst out of the hose. He swung it around and aimed it right at her.

Laughing hard, she rushed him. Any other woman would've gone screaming the other way, to get out of the spray. But not Elise. No, she rushed headlong into the situation and tried to wrestle the hose from Gabriel.

Within minutes, they were both soaked and muddy and wrestling for control of the water on the ground. Gabriel felt twenty again and foolishly in love. He let go of the hose and rolled Elise onto her back, trapping her there with his body. She smiled up at him, her face streaked with mud, her hair a wild, tangled, golden mess. She was spectacular. There would never be another woman as amazing as she was in his life.

Lowering his head to hers, he softly brushed his lips against hers. On a sigh, she opened up for him and he deepened the kiss. Within seconds, they were kissing and tearing at each other's clothes.

"Hurry," she panted as he fumbled with the buttons of her shirt. "Just rip it."

He did as she demanded and tore at the fabric of her shirt, ripping it in half and capturing her bare breasts with his mouth. He suckled on one nipple then the other, and then slowly trailed his tongue down her sternum to her navel. She giggled a little when he dipped the tip of his tongue in. She was ticklish there on her belly.

He loved her laugh, and her giggle was so sexy it drew shivers up and down his body. Nipping at her hip bones, he slid his thumbs into the band of her shorts and prepared to shuck them down her legs so he could indulge himself with other parts of her delicious body.

But before he could, her hands came on top of his head to still him. "Someone's near the cottage," she whispered.

He didn't move. "Where?" he whispered so only she could hear him.

Her gaze moved past him over his right shoulder. "Along the side, just at the edge of the yard."

"Can you tell who it is?"

She shook her head.

Releasing his hold on her pants, Gabriel slowly pulled up until he was on his hands and knees.

Before Elise could even blink again, he was turning and sprinting for the side of the house.

The trespasser must've sensed him, because he was already running back across the yard toward the woods and the road. But he wasn't fast enough.

Gabriel shifted in midrun. It took more effort and was ten times as painful as a regular shift, but he didn't have time to stop and change. Within two minutes, his clothes shredded, he was on all four furry paws chasing after the vampire who had been in the woods the previous day. He could tell by his scent.

The vampire was fast, sprinting like an Olympic athlete across the grass. But as a wolf, Gabriel was impossible to outrun.

He bounded forward and came down, catching the man around his right leg with his claws. Gabriel brought him down to the ground with a low, angry growl. The vampire screamed and kicked out at Gabriel with his other leg. He caught the wolf in the side of the head, but Gabriel didn't relinquish his hold. In fact, he dug in a little more, his claws puncturing the vampire's pants and his flesh.

"Let me go, damn it!" the vampire yelled as he punched and scratched at the wolf's face. The vampire's hat flew off in the struggle.

Gabriel opened his jaws and bared his fangs.

The vampire hissed and bared his own.

But Gabriel's were much bigger and sharper and could rip the guy's arm off in one yank.

"Fine. I give up. You win." The vampire lay back on the grass, baring his belly. It was an act of submission.

But Gabriel didn't want to let go. In fact, he had a strong urge to rip this guy to shreds. An urge that rushed down his body, making every muscle twitch and flinch in response. He opened his mouth....

"Stop." It was Elise. She had obviously found a shirt and come running after them. Alongside him now, she stroked her hand down his body. He shivered in response. "Release him."

Whining to show his displeasure, Gabriel pulled his claws from the vampire's leg and shuffled backward, giving himself room to shift back.

"I suggest you stay still," she said to the vampire.

Lucky for him, he did as he was told.

Shutting his eyes, Gabriel forced the shift through his body. After another couple of minutes, he was back in human form, shaking and covered in sweat.

He stood, but his legs shook. Elise reached out and steadied him. He nodded his thanks to her and then glared down at the fallen vampire.

"Who are you? What are you doing here?"

"Can we do this inside?" He gestured to the sun blazing down at them. "I'm getting a little hot."

Sweat was dripping down his forehead and off the end of his long nose.

"No, we're not going to do this inside. We're going to stay like this all day until you answer the damn questions," Gabriel growled.

The vampire sat up and inspected the slash in his pants. "You ruined my leg."

"You're a vamp. You'll heal. In an hour it will be like new again."

The vampire adjusted his sunglasses and fiddled with the rip in his pants.

"Answer me, asshole. Or we'll go another round."

Sighing, the vampire said, "The name's Rob, I work for the *Nouveau Monde Chronicle*."

That was when Gabriel noticed the camera that had been flung about six feet away in the grass. He walked over to it and picked it up.

"You're a reporter?" Elise asked.

He nodded. "Yeah."

"How did you find me?"

He smirked. "Funny coincidence actually. My cousin lives around here. She saw you at the market the other day and called me."

Gabriel gestured with the camera. It was a nice one, expensive, with a telephoto lens. "Did you take a bunch of pictures?"

He nodded again. "Yeah, sorry. I couldn't resist." He gave them a wry smile.

Without comment, Gabriel crushed the camera with his hands, and flung the pieces in several different directions.

The vampire jumped to his feet, wobbled a little because of his injury. "Whoa, dude. That was a three-thousand-dollar camera."

Gabriel shrugged. "Sorry. I couldn't resist."

"You son of a—"

Gabriel took a step toward him. "I'd watch yourself, Rob. You were trespassing. That's a criminal offense. I could arrest you right now."

Rob put his hand up and took a wobbly step backward. "Hey, just chill, okay. I'm cool."

"Did you tell anyone else that we were here?"

He shook his head. "No, man, once I got off the phone with my coz I jumped in my car and came here. I didn't tell anyone else, I swear."

Gabriel nodded. "Keep it that way. If I find out you're lying I will find you. Do you understand that?"

"Yeah, I totally understand."

"Now get the hell out of here."

Rob, the vampire, turned and started his long walk toward the road. He stopped and glanced over his shoulder. "I could sue you, you know, for assault and destruction of property."

"Yeah, you could try, but do you really want me to know where you live?"

Without another word, Rob continued his long walk.

Gabriel wrapped his arm around Elise, and they walked back to the house. She was shaking a little. He rubbed his hand up and down her arm, but he had a feeling that it wasn't doing any good. This had scared her.

And he had to admit, it scared him, too. If some dumb-ass vampire reporter could find them, then it was highly possible someone else could, too. And that particular someone was a lot smarter and craftier. Gabriel had a feeling they wouldn't sense him coming.

Chapter 16

Elise sighed in contentment as the hot spray of water cascaded over her head and down her face and body. She'd been shivering so badly when they got back to the house that Gabriel suggested she take a hot shower to chase the chill away.

Closing her eyes, she raised her face to the spray. It was doing its job for the most part. She was no longer cold, but there was a deep chill inside her that had nothing to do with the temperature.

Fear wound its way inside her, taking root. But it wasn't that she was afraid of her stalker; she was afraid of losing what she and Gabriel had forged together. Away from the city, away from their commitments and jobs, they were finally able to be together, something she'd been longing for longer than she even realized. And now, in this magical place, she'd been able to find him, be with him. She didn't want that to vanish, to fade away as it had all those years ago.

She feared losing him again.

"Gabriel," she called out. "Gabriel."

Two minutes later, the door to the bathroom opened and he rushed in, hands up, looking everywhere at once. "What's the matter? Are you hurt?"

She stared at him through the foggy glass shower door. He was so beautiful, so dark and dangerous, so fierce, her Gabriel. "Yes," she said. "I'm hurt."

Gabriel neared the shower door and opened it. "Where?"

She set her hand over her right breast. "Right here."

There was instant understanding in his eyes.

Pulling the door wide, he quickly shed his clothes and stepped into the stall. He shut the door behind him and moved under the hot shower with her.

"I don't want to be alone anymore," she said.

He gathered her in his arms. "You're not alone, Elise. I'll always be there for you." He pressed his body into hers, pushing her up against the side of the shower stall.

She shuddered as his scent filled her. He smelled

of grass and nature and everything she held dear. He smelled like home. A home she hadn't been to in so long.

"Kiss me."

Gabriel ran his palms down her arms and grabbed her hands, setting them on his shoulders. He pressed his hard flesh against her. Leaning down, he brushed his lips over her temple, then down her jawline.

As he peppered her face with kisses, Elise noticed the bruises blossoming along his neck and shoulders where the vampire had kicked and punched him when he'd been a wolf. They would be gone in a couple of days, but right now they were dark and black and hurt her heart. She touched the wounds, tracing her fingertips over them.

"Are they painful?"

"A little. But it was worth beating that vampire down." The corners of his mouth lifted. It was a sexy, devilish smile, so uncharacteristic of Gabriel.

She smiled with him, loving everything about him. Unable to resist him any longer, and not wanting to, she wrapped her hands around his neck and pulled him down to her lips. Warmth spread through her body, edging that ball of fear away. A bombardment of sensations coursed through her and she finally let go.

Her lips moved over his, her tongue tasting and teasing. Gabriel filled his hands with her breasts.

Her nipples hardened as he caressed them with his fingers, enjoying the way she gasped each time he moved. He gobbled up every sound she made, eager to hear more.

Desperate to feel the warmth of her skin against his, Gabriel rubbed her body with his. She responded to every movement. She was sensitive to him, to his touch. He reveled in that. He moved his fingers over her, down her torso exploring the soft dip of her waist and slope of her hip. She was so strong, yet so fragile in her own way. Her ribs tickled his palms as he stroked his way up and down her form to finally cup her with his palm.

She gasped and pulled back from his kiss. "Gabriel. I want you so much."

"Then you can have me," he growled as he looked down at her.

Her eyes fluttered closed as he massaged her nipples with one hand and stroked her hard between the thighs with the other. He loved the lost look on her face. One of abandonment, of complete surrender.

"You're so damn beautiful."

As he caressed her, he looked her over from head to toe, drinking in his fill of her magnificent body. She was so striking, powerful, with sculpted muscles and sleek lines. His breathtaking blood wolf.

He couldn't hold himself back any longer. His desire was ripping at him, clawing its way out. He needed to have her, possess her utterly. Both his beasts inside would accept nothing less. Both lycan and vampire screamed at him to take her.

Growling low in his throat, he wrapped his arms around her and crushed his mouth to hers. The powerful kiss left him reeling and dizzy. Gabriel trailed his hands down her back and molded the firm cheeks of her butt, and then he picked her up, settling her firmly against the stall wall. Instinctively, she opened her legs and wrapped them around him. Gripping her tight in his arms, he nipped on her bottom lip and made his way over her chin to her neck. Her wet skin was like ambrosia on his tongue.

He nuzzled in between her legs, effectively pinning her with his body. With the heat of her center pressed against his erection, Gabriel thought he'd died and gone to heaven. Surely, Elise was his angel.

His whole body trembled with pent-up desire, a ferocious, insatiable hunger. He needed to be inside her now. He would waste away to nothing if he had to wait much longer without having her completely and wholly.

"I've been lost without you, Elise," he growled into her ear, after licking the side of her neck. "I won't go another second without you with me."

"I'm yours. Forever." Her lips pressed together tightly. He could feel her body quivering under his touch. The smell of her desire enveloped him. It was an exotic spice. The smell of pure perfection. The scent of his love.

He nipped at her chin and rocked his hips, grinding his shaft into her warmth. His arms shook with strain and repressed need. He couldn't hold back for much longer. But he'd gone so many years without her, he wanted every second to count.

With one hand, he sought her liquid heat. She was hot and wet and ready. His restraint vanishing, he guided himself in between her legs. With one swift thrust, he buried his entire length inside.

Every nerve ending in his body sparked to life as he moved slowly at first, and then picked up his pace before finding a delicious rhythm that sent shivers from his toes to his scalp.

He'd had other lovers before, but he had never felt so alive with them. With Elise, it was as if the world only existed for them. Nothing else mattered.

As he slid in and out of her, the wild part of him howled inside his head. Sensing Elise's beast, it longed to be released. It wanted to mate. It sensed its partner in her.

As if recognizing his needs, her thighs squeezed against his waist and she pulled at his shoulders to bring him closer. But he was as close as he could get without actually stepping inside her body.

Bringing his hand up, he stroked her cheek and buried his face into the slope of her neck. Her scent was strong here, and he could hear the rush of her blood through her veins. His vampire side urged him to bite her, to taste her blood. But Gabriel pushed that primal part of himself back.

Digging her fingers into his shoulders, she found his mouth with hers and kissed with eagerness, nibbling and teasing his tongue. A growl rumbled out of her as he buried a hand in her hair and countered with his own tasting of her mouth.

He pounded between her legs as they kissed. With each thrust, Gabriel thought he'd go mad with pleasure. It didn't just ripple over his skin but surged through every inch of his body.

Streaking her hands to his back, she seemed to search for purpose, something to hang on to as he took her up, pushing them both close to the edge of orgasm. Shifting his stance, he gripped her butt cheeks tight, pushed her hard against the wall and buried himself deep.

Gasping, she dug her nails into his flesh and raked them across his back. Gabriel returned her fervor by clamping down on her shoulder with his teeth. Moaning, she urged him on as she bucked and writhed against his body.

"More," he growled while licking the spot on her collarbone where he had just bitten. "I want more."

"Take it," she groaned. "Take it all."

Opening his mouth wide, he felt tiny fangs distend from his gums. For the first time in his life, he sank those fangs into her flesh and tasted her blood.

It was a shock at first, hot and tangy, but then he savored the flavor and drank her in. He only took a little, as that was all he desired, and then he pressed his tongue on the wounds and closed them.

Elise was panting hard when he glanced up into her face. She opened her eyes, met his gaze and smiled at him. "That was indescribable. I never knew it would feel like that."

"Did I hurt you?"

"Yes, and it was delicious." She threw her head back and laughed.

Settling her in his arms, Gabriel kicked open the shower door and carried her into the bedroom. She squeezed her thighs tight around his waist and held on, but that didn't stop her from feasting on his lips, groaning into his mouth with each stride of his powerful legs.

When he reached the bed, he placed her on the mattress and, growling, gazed down at her with wild fire in his eyes. She met his with her own hot intense gaze that made his stomach flip and his thighs clench. No one had ever looked at him like that. Wild, feral, lost to the pleasure whipping around them both in hot, fiery lashes.

She reached out for him, gripping him around the waist, and pulled him to her. She touched his stomach, trailing her fingers around his navel. His muscles flinched and quivered under her touch. She had power over him and she knew it.

Urging him closer, Elise pressed her lips to his sternum and licked her way down to his belly button and back up again. He moaned and wrapped his hands in her hair. Tilting her head, he stared down at her. He could feel the muscles in his jaw twitching with the barely controlled passion surging through him like a tornado.

"You drive me mad, woman."

She smiled at him and dug her fingers into his backside, taunting him further.

Gabriel took the challenge and pulled her up to his hungry mouth. He kissed her hard, devouring her lips with teeth and tongue. In return she nibbled on his bottom lip and then moaned into his mouth, "Take me completely."

He needed no more encouragement.

Breaking the kiss, he spun her around and pushed her forward on the mattress. She put out her hands in time to break her fall, but she didn't have time to do anything else before he was pressing up against her backside, his legs in between hers, moving them apart. His hands clamped down around her hips, preventing any attempt at escape. She belonged to him completely.

He nuzzled his erection into the juncture of her

parted thighs. Digging her fingers into the mattress, Elise bit down on her lip as he slowly entered her, inch by inch. She writhed against him, forcing him in even further.

Once sheathed fully inside her, Gabriel start to move, rotating his hips, filling her with each stroke. With every thrust forward she pushed back, meeting him, matching his rhythm. Pleasure swelled over him, through him. All thought and reason vanished from his mind. He was too enthralled to do anything but hang on as he pushed into her without cause, without reason.

She closed her eyes and moaned as he fell forward onto her back, wrapping his hands around her body, filling his palms with her breasts as he buried himself deep. He could barely breathe as he continued to slide in and out of her. He moved one hand down and cupped her where they joined. Two fingers slipped over her creamy silk, circling the sensitive bundle of nerves at her center. As he pressed one then two fingers down on her, he could feel her orgasm building and knew she'd come soon, just as he would.

His thighs tightened, and his breath hitched in his throat just as she cried out his name and tore at the sheets beneath her. As if in an attempt to escape her pleasure Elise tried to crawl away from him, but Gabriel held her down with his body, coaxing more from her with his clever fingers and his tongue on the back of her neck. She quivered uncontrollably and cried out just as Gabriel shuddered above her and, hugging her tightly, lost himself to his own orgasm.

Chapter 17

"We found the driver."

Gabriel ran a hand through his messy hair as he stood on the deck of Elise's bedroom and looked across the yard toward the trees. Sophie had called, so he'd slipped on his jeans and padded out to the deck. He didn't want Elise to hear the call.

"And?"

"Looks like suicide."

"But, you don't think so."

"No. It's too convenient. I don't like it."

"What was the method?" As he leaned on the railing, he glanced over his shoulder to make sure Elise was still in bed. She was, her slender naked back to him.

"He was found hanging in his apartment."

"Any sign of forced entry?"

"No. And there are no marks on his body. Nothing to indicate he didn't stand on the chair, toss up the rope and hang himself."

"Any suicide note?"

"Yeah. 'I didn't mean it.' Which, to me, covers just about anything, including I didn't mean to hang myself."

"You have a gut feeling about this?" he asked. Sophie was a good investigator with strong intuitions. He trusted them.

"Yeah."

Sighing, he ran his hand through his hair again. "Okay, do what you have to. Make sure to run a tox screen. Do you need me there?"

"Nah, you're doing what you need to do there. Keeping Ms. Leroy safe. Because I honestly believe she's in danger."

He nodded. "Yeah, I do, too."

"I'll keep you updated."

"Yeah, okay." He pushed away from the railing. "Oh, hey, can you do me a favor?"

"Anything."

"Could you find out anything about a Rob that works at the *Chronicle?* He was out here taking pictures. I guess he has a cousin in a hamlet nearby who saw us."

"What do you want me to do with him if I find him?"

"Just keep an eye on him and what he's writing in the *Chronicle*. I told him to keep his mouth shut or bad things would happen to him. But you know how some reporters can be."

"You got it, Gabe. Anything else?"

"Just do your job well, you know?"

"I know."

"And keep me in the loop."

"No problem."

"Talk to you soon." He flipped his phone closed and gritted his teeth. God, he hated not being able to do his job. To dive into the investigation and find and collect the evidence. He felt like a complete failure standing here on this deck looking out at this beautiful scenery as if on a grand holiday. He felt he was failing his team.

He was still gazing across the yard, frustrated and angry, when Elise came up from behind and wrapped her arms around him, pressing a kiss to the back of his shoulder.

"What a gorgeous day."

He didn't respond.

She moved around him so she could see his face. "What's wrong?"

He didn't know if he should tell her. He didn't want to scare her, but maybe that was what she needed, so she could finally realize how much danger she was really in. Then maybe she would listen to him when he told her to do something or not do something. He did it for her safety. Always to keep her safe.

"Your driver supposedly hung himself. They found his body."

Her eyes narrowed. "But you don't believe that. You think he was murdered."

"Sophie doesn't buy the suicide. She's looking into all the possibilities."

"You think this has something to do with me."

"I don't believe in coincidences."

Pursing her lips, she turned to lean on the railing and look across the expanse of the yard. "Do you think he was murdered by the same person who's after me?"

"My team is going over all the evidence."

She whirled around. "I'm not asking about the evidence, I'm asking what you think, what you honestly believe."

He rubbed his hands up and down her arms. "I believe you're in danger."

She looked at him for a long moment. "Well, we already knew that, right? That's why you're here. To keep me safe."

He wanted to tell her that it was more than that. That he'd agreed to come because of more than his need to protect her. He carried deep-seated emotions for her. Emotions that crippled him sometimes.

For now he just nodded, and brought one hand up to her shoulder. He ran his fingers over the bite marks he'd given her.

"Do they hurt?"

She shook her head, but he could see in her eyes that something else did. She pulled away from his touch. "I'll go fix us something to eat. How about crepes?"

Nodding, he let her go, when what he really wanted to do was wrap her in his arms and take her back to bed. He knew what he was doing there. It was between that and his job that he was lost. He didn't know how to be just Gabriel with her. Especially when he wasn't too certain just who the real Gabriel Bellmonte was. Protector? Lover? Friend? The question was, could he be all three to her and not lose himself in the end?

Elise pulled open the refrigerator and grabbed the egg carton. She proceeded to crack three eggs into a bowl, pretending the egg was Gabriel's head.

She was trying hard not to think about the things she knew he wasn't telling her. He'd always been like that. *Do as I say, but I'm not going to tell you why.* He was a stubborn jerk sometimes with a thick skull.

Yes, she could be stubborn, as well. She always thought she could protect herself. She was tough and resourceful and never counted on anyone to do something for her. Especially not something she could do herself.

But despite her complaints about the situation, now she knew she needed help. She knew there was a threat looming. Still, Gabriel didn't have to treat her like a child. She was a grown woman who could rip out a man's throat if need be. Her sangloup genes gave her that kind of power. She definitely wasn't defenseless, even if Gabriel liked to treat her as such.

Elise added the salt and sugar and butter, and then moved to the refrigerator for milk. The milk jug was empty.

Tying her robe tighter around her waist, she went across the kitchen to the front door. Hopefully the milkman had already visited. It was late in the morning so she thought he would have.

The moment she twisted the knob on the door and pulled it open she knew there was something wrong. She could smell it in the air before she could even consider what it was.

The stench of death was unfathomable, but it was all the blood that dropped her to her knees. The front porch was awash in crimson. Flies congregated in it, as if around an office watercooler, drinking their fill. But it was the glassy dead eyes of the gutted wolf staring into her that made her freeze with fear.

  She screamed.

Chapter 18

Gabriel was there in three seconds flat, hugging her close. He must've sprinted through the house, finding her crouched on the floor, her back to the wall. He rocked her and stroked a hand over her hair.

"It's okay. I got you."

"That poor animal," she sobbed. She'd seen death before. As a wolf, she'd even inflicted her own upon rabbits and squirrels and other small game, but this...

This was a cold-blooded massacre.

There was rage and ruthlessness and hate behind this killing. And the message was clear.

"I've got to check it out, baby." He kissed the top

of her head, then stood and turned to go out the door and onto the porch. "I'll be right back."

She watched him as he stepped gingerly onto the porch, taking care to not step in the blood. He surveyed the scene and then returned.

"I need to get my kit from the car. The scene is fairly fresh, so the blood hasn't congealed too much. I'd say this was done a couple of hours ago max."

She shivered at that and pulled her knees closer to her chest.

"I'm going to call it in and get a team here." He touched her head to get her attention. "Do you hear me, Elise? I'm going out back and around to the car."

She glanced up at him and nodded that she understood. He smoothed his hand over her hair then walked toward the kitchen to go out into the backyard.

She didn't know how long she sat there against the wall, arms wrapped around her body. Time seemed irrelevant. The front door was open, the bloody scene in her peripheral vision. She didn't know if she'd ever get that smell out of her nose. Death had a habit of hanging around a lot longer than a person wanted. It was something she'd never forget for the rest of her life.

By the time anything started to register, Gabriel was back, standing in front of her. He reached down and grabbed her arms, pulling her to her feet. With an arm around her shoulders, he guided her into the living room and down onto the sofa. Once there, he wrapped her with a blanket and went back into the kitchen. He came back with a steaming cup of tea.

He put it in her stiff hands. "Drink it. It'll help ease the shock a little."

She took a sip, then another, and another, until the entire drink was gone. She felt a little better, warmer, and not so brittle cold. When she set the cup down, Gabriel sat down beside her, near enough that she could grab on to him if she wanted, but far enough away to allow her the illusion of independence.

"My team will get here as fast as they can. An hour and a half I'd say if Sophie's driving."

She nodded and then looked out the big bay window at the front of the villa. It was turning into a beautiful sunny day. It almost made her sick to see that.

She turned back to Gabriel. "Who would do something like that?"

"Someone who's unstable. Whoever did this has some serious mental problems. And those instabilities are focused on you. It was no coincidence that the animal was a wolf."

She got that loud and clear.

"I want to do another sweep around the villa and see if I can pick up any scents, or maybe even get lucky and find a footprint."

She nodded.

"But I don't want to leave you unless you're okay." He grabbed her hand and squeezed it.

She looked into his face. She could see he was really trying to be there for her, when what he wanted to do was go and investigate and collect the evidence and solve the crime. He was good at his job, and she knew he'd solve this one. He'd find the person responsible for this terrible thing. He'd bring him to justice.

"Go do your job. I'll be fine. I just need to sit here for a while and breathe."

He smoothed a hand over her hair and then bent forward to kiss her on the top of her head. "I won't be long. Just a search of the area. I'll have the house in view the whole time."

He stood, and she watched him go out the back again. When he was gone, she pulled the blanket up tighter around her chin and snuggled down into the comforting cushions of the sofa. It should've been a good day, a relaxing day full of sun and comfort and love. But now all she could think about was that death had come to her door. And he wasn't going away anytime soon.

Gabriel walked around the house twice before taking up a stance near the porch at the front. He didn't notice any unfamiliar footprints near the house. He recognized his own and Elise's and that was it. So whoever had done this had approached from the front.

The house was isolated, trees all around, the main road hidden by a long driveway and more trees. So it was possible for the perpetrator to carry the wolf and gut it on the porch in plain view. There were no blood drops off the porch, so it made sense that was what he had done. The perp probably caught and killed the animal in the woods, then carried it here to do his work.

But that would mean the perp had to have been covered in blood. There was a mess on the porch. There was no way someone gutted the wolf and walked away clean. It would've been impossible.

Gabriel walked around the porch, examining it from every direction. He looked along the edge of the wood and the grass around it. There had to be blood drops somewhere. The perp couldn't have just vanished. He didn't know of any Otherworlder that possessed that kind of power. Not even an ancient, pure-blooded vampire.

And that was when he spotted two small drops on the underside of the railing along the porch.

He examined them and then glanced directly down into the grass. Crouching, he pushed aside some blades, looking at the ground. There was another drop, no larger than a button. He rushed back to his crime-scene kit, took out the stack of plastic numbers and returned to the site. He set down a number one next to the first blood drop. Still crouching, he moved along the grass line, and found another small drop about four feet from the first one. He set another plastic card down. Then he found another six feet away. The line was going in a northerly direction right through the trees that lined the road leading to the cottage.

Leaning his face down to the latest blood drop, his nose an inch above it, he inhaled deeply. If he could catch the scent maybe he could follow it that way instead of on his hands and knees brushing through the tall grass. Closing his eyes, he took in another breath then another, until finally he could identify the smell beyond the others in the field.

Standing, he raised his nose and caught the scent almost immediately. Then he started to run. Within minutes, he was through the trees and to the gravel road. He followed the scent along the ditch until it just stopped. Obviously the perp had had a vehicle waiting for him. He set another plastic marker along the ditch.

Crouching down again, Gabriel examined the road looking for tire treads. Maybe he'd get lucky and find one that they could mold and match in a tire-tread website. But after another fifteen minutes of looking, he couldn't find any distinguishable patterns.

His cell phone rang from his pants pocket. He slid it out and flipped it open. "Bellmonte."

"We'll be there in forty-five minutes max."

Shaking his head, he pushed through the trees again to head back to the house. "Forty-five minutes? You must be traveling, at what, one hundred and forty?"

Sophie chuckled. "Give or take ten kilometers."

"Okay, see you then." He flipped the phone closed, and walked the rest of the way back to the cottage.

He decided he should check on Elise. But as he passed the porch to head around back, another scent wafted to his nose. It had the odor of something familiar. Spiced blood. It was a vampire smell, but it was a bit different. And he was sure he'd smelled it before.

Jogging now, he ran around to the back, onto the deck and through the open kitchen door. "Elise," he called.

He went into the living room where he'd left her. She wasn't there. Just the blanket she'd been wrapped in lay on the floor.

"Elise!" he yelled. Swinging around the room, he took deep breaths of air. Her scent was still strong. She'd been here only moments before.

Heart racing, he rushed down the hall to her room. She wasn't there. Panic made his head swim. Then he heard the sound of rushing water. He moved through the bedroom into the bathroom and saw her in the shower.

Still in her robe, she was sitting with her back to one of the walls. Water pounded down on her. As he approached, he could see that she had her face in her hands, resting them on her bent knees.

He pulled open the shower door. She looked up at him, her face wet, her hair sticking to her cheeks and forehead. The broken expression on her face nearly knocked him over.

"The smell of death won't come out," she said matter-of-factly as she picked up her sodden silk robe and showed it to him.

Gabriel reached down and grabbed her hand in his. She was shaking badly. Keeping her hand in his, he came into the shower stall and sat down beside her. He wrapped his arm around her shoulders and pulled her close to him. He nuzzled his face into her wet hair, trying hard to keep his emotions in check. It wouldn't do her any good to see him rattled, to see him nearly broken apart by her pain and despair.

"I won't let anything happen to you, baby. I'll keep you safe."

She wrapped her arms around him and buried her face in his chest. Even though he couldn't feel or see the tears on her face, he knew she was crying. Her whole body shook with the power of her despair.

He rocked her and mumbled soothing words to her until the water ran cold.

Chapter 19

Sophie snapped off a few more pictures, and then lowered the camera. "Wow. That's a whole hell of a lot of rage right there. Someone's really pissed off."

"Yeah," Gabriel agreed.

"I wonder what set him off?"

That was exactly what he'd been trying to figure out. Something in the past few days had triggered the anger and rage in this stalker. He'd escalated big-time. And something inside Gabriel told him the stalker was male.

"Maybe he figured the two of you were, you know, getting acquainted." She arched her eyebrow as she said it.

Gabriel didn't respond but he figured he didn't have to.

Sophie shrugged. "It's written all over your face, boss. Plus—" she tapped her nose "—I have the best nose on this team. I could've scented the pheromones running rampant in this house from down the road."

He frowned, and walked back into the house. He found Elise sitting in the kitchen, teacup in hand, giving her statement to Constable Ronald Sharpe, who'd ridden up here with Sophie. He was a good cop.

She smiled when she saw him come through the door. "Coffee, Gabriel?"

He shook his head. "Can I have a minute with her, Ron?"

The constable stood. "Of course. I'm going to need your statement as well, Inspector."

"I know."

When Ron had gone out the way Gabriel had come in, he turned to Elise. "Have you talked to anyone in the past two days?"

"Just Lily."

"Did you tell her about—" he pursed his lips, unsure on how to phrase it "—about us?"

"Of course not." She set her cup down. "She's a smart girl, though. I imagine she doesn't need to be told."

He ran a hand through his hair. "Anyone else?"

"No. I had Lily relay whatever information needed to be relayed to my publicist and agent."

"Is she still seeing Diego?"

Elise ran her finger along the teacup. "I don't know. She said she'd break it off, but that doesn't mean she did right away."

He sighed, and then sat in the chair vacated by the constable.

"Why the questions? Did you find something?"

"I caught a scent near the porch. It's vampire."

"Maybe our paparazzi friend returned."

He shook his head. "I had Sophie put a tail on him. He hasn't left the city. Besides, I think I recognize the smell."

Her eyes widened then. "You don't think Diego…"

"I don't know what to think, but I need to find out."

"What do you suggest?" she asked, but by the lost look in her eyes, he suspected she already knew what he had in mind.

"I'm going back into the city. I have to follow this lead to the end." He reached across the table and grabbed her hand. "Sophie and I will go back and Constable Sharpe will stay here with you. I trust him. He's a good cop."

She nodded. "Okay."

He squeezed her hand. "This will be all over soon, I promise."

She just nodded again. Her hand still in his, Gabriel stood and came around to the other side. He pulled her up into his arms and hugged her tight. He nuzzled his face into her neck.

"You're going to be fine. In a few weeks, this will be all just a bad dream, and everything will go back to normal."

"Maybe I don't want normal back."

He pulled away and looked into her face. "What are you saying?"

"I don't know, exactly. But I can't deny that these past few days with you have been my happiest." She sighed. "I haven't felt the pressure and stress of being in the spotlight. I could just be me, Elise, simple farm girl. I can be just me when I'm with you. I like how that feels, Gabriel."

"But you aren't that simple farm girl anymore. This is the life you've chosen. And you're remarkable at what you do."

She ran a hand up his back to his neck. She played her fingers though his hair. "But what if I wanted to *unchoose* it? Would you be there for me? Would you wait until I could sort it all out?"

He wanted to answer her, but in all honesty he wasn't sure what his answer was. He'd been waiting for her for fifteen years. Where was she then?

"We don't have to talk about this now."

"I think we do, Gabriel. I feel like now is the perfect time."

He pulled back a little. "Once this is over we can talk about it, if you want. Right now, I have to wrap up this crime scene and get back to the city."

She dropped her arms and stepped out of his embrace. "Fine. Go do your job."

"I'll call you when I get into the city."

She didn't say anything, just looked at him over the rim of the cup she'd picked back up and sipped from. "Please do."

He could feel the arctic reach of her anger. She was angry at him for not stopping everything to talk about their relationship. It wasn't that he didn't want to discuss it—he did—it was just it was not the right time. He had other things on his mind, like solving this case and keeping her safe from harm.

But he didn't think telling her that would diminish her anger. Communication had always been a problem between them. They came at a conversation from two completely different angles. Unfortunately, those angles just didn't add up to anything positive.

"We'll be packing up and taking the body with us. When we're gone, I'll have Constable Sharpe clean up the porch, so you don't have to see or smell it anymore."

"The smell will never go away, no matter how much cleanser he uses."

He nodded. He understood what she meant. No one could wipe the sight from her mind. It would stay in there, possibly for the rest of her life. He knew what that was like. He lived with that every day as part of his job. There had been crime scenes in his time that he wished he could erase from his psyche. This one, here at Elise's cottage, was one of them.

It brought out too many emotions in him, fear and anger being at the forefront. Fear for Elise. Fear for her life. And anger for the fact that he hadn't been able to keep her from the ugliness of it. It had come to her door right under his nose, and he hadn't sensed its approach.

"I'll call you. Stay in the house. Don't go out running." He was gone before she could respond.

He came around the house to stand next to Sophie. She'd just finished bagging and tagging some evidence. She glanced briefly at him. "So, what's the word, boss?"

"We're taking the body in and then we're making a house call."

"You look like a man with an idea."

He nodded. "I've caught a scent that's familiar. I need to check it out."

Sophie snapped her crime-scene kit closed, then stripped off her latex gloves, shoved them into her pocket and pulled on another pair.

"Okay, let's do this." She handed him a pair of plastic covers for his shoes. "Do you want the head or the tail?"

Ignoring her question, Gabriel snapped on the gloves, put on shoe protectors and stepped up onto the porch. Sophie came over with a plastic sheet. As gently as they could, they lowered the carcass onto the sheet, and he wrapped it up, sealing it closed with duct tape. Then they picked up the plastic roll and carried it down to the lab's SUV Sophie had driven down in.

Once that was done, Gabriel stripped off the gloves and plastic on his feet and called Constable Sharpe over.

"No one comes near this house. I don't care who it is. You get me?"

Ron nodded. "I get you."

"And she doesn't leave. No matter what. You have to be firm on that. She'll push you, but be firm."

"Right. Be firm with a world-famous movie star." He smirked.

"I'm serious, Ron."

"I know. I'll do everything in my power to keep her safe."

"Thank you. I know you will."

With a final handshake with Ron, Gabriel went to the vehicle to get in. Turning, he looked at the house and saw Elise standing at the big bay window in front. Smiling, he lifted his hand to her.

She waved back.

A sudden urge to go to her surged through him. He wanted to hold her close and never let go. A sense of dread needled him. As if this would be the last time he'd see her. It was a ridiculous notion, but he couldn't shake it.

Sucking it up, he opened the car door and slid in, then leaned back in the seat. But he knew he wouldn't relax on the drive. He didn't think he'd ever be able to relax again. Not until this guy was put down. One way or another.

Chapter 20

When Gabriel was gone, Elise wandered back into the kitchen. She took her teacup, dumped the now-cold contents and set it into the sink, intending to wash it and the other dirty dishes. But she couldn't get the image of the gutted wolf out of her mind.

It saddened and sickened her. To think someone could do that. And it scared her to think that Gabriel suspected Diego.

Could it be him?

He certainly had a temper. And he was a full-blown narcissist. He loved to be the center of attention. Also, the letters did start coming not long after they broke up. And the breakup had been a very public event outing him as a cheater, a liar and an all-around nasty person. Was this all a revenge thing?

She shivered, thinking that at one time she'd had real feelings for him. And that they'd had sex. She tried to remember if there had been anything deviant in his sexual behavior.

Oh, my God. She had to call Lily. She had to get the girl as far away from Diego as she could. If he was the one, then he'd been using Lily for information to find ways to get to her.

Elise picked up the phone lying on the counter and dialed Lily's number. Thankfully, she answered on the third ring. "Hey, Elise."

"Where are you?"

"Having a late lunch with a friend."

"You're not with Diego, are you?"

"No, of course not." Elise could hear noises in the background, the sounds of people chattering. "I actually haven't heard from him in days."

"Lily, listen to me. This is very important. You have to promise me you won't call Diego or see him."

"Okay." Elise could hear the hesitation in Lily's voice. "Why? What's going on?"

"Just promise me."

"I promise."

"Thank you."

"Everything okay, there? Is the inspector pissing you off?"

Elise chuckled. "Everything's fine. And the inspector is behaving himself."

"Somehow I doubt that."

"Enjoy your lunch, Lily. I'll see you soon." She hung up the phone and set it back onto the counter. She felt a little better now that Lily had been warned. The girl was smart, she'd listen to Elise.

Constable Sharpe came into the house. "Ms. Leroy, I'm going to clean up the mess out front now. Do you have any garbage bags?"

Elise turned and reached under the sink. She grabbed a green plastic bag and handed it to him. "You can call me Elise, Constable Sharpe."

Smiling, he took the bag. "And you call me Ron."

"All right, Ron. While you do that horrible job, I'm going to make you some lunch."

"There's really no need."

"Yes, there is." She smiled. "I feel better when I cook."

"Well, then, cook away. I can always eat." He patted his flat stomach, and then headed out with the bag to the front porch. She noticed he stopped to put plastic coverings on his shoes.

She turned away from the door and opened the refrigerator. She would make a tomato mozzarella salad to start and then go from there. She grabbed the mozzarella then, closing the door, she turned to retrieve the tomatoes fresh from her garden and sitting in a bowl.

Grabbing the cutting board and knife, she started to slice the tomatoes, hoping the chore would take her mind off the blood on her front porch. Then she cut up the cheese and, adding salt and pepper, alternated layers of them in a big bowl. She added fresh basil and olive oil.

Pleased, she set the colorful dish on the counter and went to call Ron. She thought they both needed a break and some mutual company.

She moved toward the front door hesitantly. She didn't really want another gander at the bloody mess. "Ron." She poked her head out. "Ron, I've made a salad." He wasn't on the porch.

He must've gone around back for the water hose to spray off the blood. It would've been the easier way to clean the area. She turned to go find Ron, intending to check the patio, when the sliding glass door slid open and a figure loomed in the doorway.

Elise was startled and put her hand to her throat. "What are you doing here?"

Chapter 21

After they dropped the dead wolf at the lab, Sophie and Gabriel went to the soundstage where Elise had been working. Since filming had been halted due to her absence, there wasn't a lot of traffic in and out. But there were some people around, including the director.

When he saw Gabriel, Sophie beside him, Reginald smiled and came toward them. "Nice to see you, Inspector. How is Elise?"

"She's fine. I was hoping I could have access to Diego Martinez's trailer."

Reginald frowned. "Of course. May I inquire why?"

"I'm following a lead."

He nodded and yelled for an assistant. "I need a key to the trailers."

A young, pimply faced man ran over to Reginald's side and showed him a key ring. Reginald gestured for them to follow him to the back lot where the talent trailers were. He pointed toward one, somewhat smaller than Elise's had been. Gabriel bet that had pricked Diego's ass.

"Have you seen Diego in the past few days?"

The director shook his head. "Since we are down for a bit, I gave all the actors time off." He gestured for the kid to open the trailer. He did, then left.

"How would you describe Diego's feelings toward Elise?"

Reginald snorted. "Combative."

"Would you classify them as hostile?"

The director frowned. "Hostile? No. There are definite bad feelings between them, because of their nasty breakup and the fact that Diego is a rather unpleasant person to begin with. But I wouldn't say he was hostile toward her. He'd never hurt her, if that is what you are inferring."

"Thank you." Gabriel stepped up to the trailer and opened the door. "If I have any other questions I will come find you."

"Of course." Reginald walked away looking very nervous. He was probably thinking about the ramifications on his film if Diego turned out to be the stalker. Although, Gabriel thought, in this society, that kind of publicity could transform the movie into a blockbuster.

If Diego turned out to be Elise's nemesis, many would want to see the film that had driven him to his madness. It wouldn't surprise Gabriel if another movie was made—about him and his obsession.

He stepped up into the trailer. It indicated what type of person Diego was. Narcissistic came to mind. There were at least seven mirrors on the walls, one huge one in the corner, near that a table and chair, with many grooming products on it.

"Wow, I thought Kellen had a fascination with looking at himself in mirrors. This guy is something."

Gabriel nodded. "Yeah, something." He walked into the middle of the trailer and took in a deep breath. He did it again and again until he caught Diego's signature scent.

It was the same as at the cottage. Diego had definitely been there. Had he killed a wolf and gutted it on the porch? That, Gabriel couldn't be sure of, but he was going to track the star down and find out.

"What's the word, boss?"

"Let's search it. I don't think he'd be stupid enough to leave any incriminating evidence, but I'd hate to miss something when we had access to it." Gabriel slid his phone out of his pocket. "I'm going to call and get a warrant for his house."

An hour later, he and Sophie had searched the trailer and had a warrant for Diego's house. Now they just had to track him down.

They drove to his home, a fifteen-thousand-square-foot estate with two acres of land around it. Of course there was a gate and a guard.

Gabriel flashed the badge. "We need to speak with Diego Martinez."

"He's unavailable," the guard said through the intercom.

"I have a warrant to search the premises." He held up the papers. "Please open the gate and have someone meet us at the front door."

After a few minutes, the gate swung open and Sophie drove the SUV through and parked in the circular driveway near the front entrance. Once parked, they got out and walked to the main door. It opened and a vampiress in a red power suit loomed in the doorway.

"I'm Gloria, Mr. Martinez's personal assistant. How can I be of service?"

Gabriel handed her the warrant papers. "I'm Inspector Bellmonte and I have a warrant to search the premises."

"What is this about?"

"When was the last time you saw Mr. Martinez?"

"Yesterday."

"What time?"

"We had lunch."

"Where and when?" He pulled out the notebook he always carried.

She gave him the details, and then, obviously angry at the intrusion, led them through the house to Diego's office so they could do their job.

"Do you live here with Mr. Martinez?" he asked.

"No."

"Then I take it you have a key to his house."

"Of course. I take care of everything for Diego. I was just here dealing with some of his appointments when you arrived."

"Okay. If I have more questions, I'll find you."

In a huff, she walked away, high heels clicking. When she was gone, Gabriel said to Sophie, "You start in here. I'm going to find his bedroom."

As Gabriel left the study, his cell phone rang. He flipped it open. "Bellmonte."

"Inspector, this is Lily May Jones."

"Yes, Lily." Gabriel shut his eyes and silently cursed at himself. He'd completely forgotten to call Elise when he got to the city. He'd have to do that once this call was done.

"I thought you'd want to know where Diego Martinez is. I talked to Elise today and she made me promise not to see him so I just figured maybe something was up with him."

"I'm listening."

"He's at La Lune de Sang on Fifth Avenue with his new girlfriend."

Gabriel knew the place. It was an upscale trendy restaurant that catered to the rich and famous.

"So, what, you're mad at him for replacing you and you're getting back at him?"

"No. I love Elise, and if Diego's hurt her, then yeah, I want revenge."

"Duly noted. Thanks for the tip." He flipped the phone closed and returned to the office. Sophie was busy rifling through the desk drawers. "Anything interesting?"

She shook her head. "Just the usual papers. Contracts and such."

"Keep at it. I'm heading downtown. Got a tip where Diego might be."

"Good."

"I'll send someone over to help you."

"Okay. Later." She went back to her search. He could always count on Sophie to do her job efficiently and thoroughly.

As he walked through the house, he took out his phone and called Elise on her cell. It rang five times before clicking over to her voice mail.

"Elise, are you there? Please call me back." He

flipped the phone closed. Nerves settled in him. Maybe she was just out in the garden and had neglected to take her phone. He tried Ron's cell. His voice mail picked up immediately. And maybe Ron was out front cleaning up the porch, as he'd asked him to. He'd try again in ten minutes.

Ten minutes later he was on his way downtown to La Lune de Sang. He called Elise again. Another five rings without an answer. He left another message. "I need you to call me back the second you get this."

He set his phone down and noticed a slight tremble to his fingers. He flexed his hand and clamped it back onto the steering wheel. There had to be an explanation for why she wasn't answering. He couldn't read anything nefarious into it.

He parked in a no-park zone in front of the restaurant, got out and went inside. The maître d' met him at the door, looking him up and down, likely taking in his faded trench coat and the scruff on his chin.

"May I help you, sir?"

Gabriel flipped him the get-in-free badge. "Diego Martinez."

The man lifted his eyebrows but said nothing as he led him to a table in the corner of the restaurant. Diego was there with a buxom redhead whom Gabriel recognized as Layla Lee, an upcoming "It" girl.

She was all vampire. Unabashedly so with her fangs out on display at all times.

Diego saw him as he approached the table. He smiled, but Gabriel could tell it was forced. "Inspector Bellmonte, right?"

"I need to ask you a few questions."

Diego glanced at his lady friend, then steepled his fingers on the table. "Go ahead."

"We need to do it downtown at the station."

He leaned back in his chair and smirked. "Is that really necessary?"

"Yes, it is."

"Could I finish my meal at least?"

Gabriel shook his head. "No. Now, you can come with me or I can call in a uniform with a car that has flashing lights and we can make a huge scene. It's up to you. But either way you're coming downtown to answer some questions."

Diego glanced around the restaurant. From the corner of Gabriel's eye, he noticed there was already a lot of attention directed toward the table.

Sighing, Diego stood and tossed his linen napkin onto the table. "I can't believe this."

Layla jumped to her feet. "What's going on, Diego?"

He leaned over to press his lips to her temple. "I'm sorry, darling. Something's come up. I'll call you later and we can pick this up where we left off."

She huffed. "Not likely. I've got better things to do than wait around for you."

"Fine. Your loss."

Gabriel walked out of the restaurant, Diego in tow. When they were outside, Gabriel opened the back door for him.

A couple of paparazzi sprang into action, taking pictures while Diego waved to them as if he was getting into a limo after one of his movie premieres instead of heading down to the police station for questioning.

"Damn Elise for putting me through this. She's always been a pain in my ass," Diego mumbled, but Gabriel heard every word.

So when he was helping Diego into the car, it was no mistake when he knocked the vampire's head into the top of the door frame. When he turned to protest, Gabriel shoved him hard into the seat and slammed the door shut, nearly crushing the actor's leg in the process.

The paparazzi jumped on him then. "Is Diego Martinez under arrest?" one asked.

Another shouted, "Is this in connection with Elise Leroy's stalker case?"

"No comment," Gabriel said as he came around the vehicle and got into the driver's seat. He shut the door on the plethora of questions being tossed out.

"I could sue you for police brutality."

Gabriel turned and glared at him. "You haven't seen police brutality—I could show you if you like."

"I'm calling my lawyer." He flipped open his phone and dialed while looking out the side window.

As Gabriel pulled away from the curb and into the street he flipped his phone open again and dialed Elise's number. Again it rang five times and he got her voice mail. "Are you punishing me? Just call me back, okay. I don't care if you *are* mad at me." He flipped the phone closed.

"Trouble in paradise," Diego chimed in.

Gabriel declined to respond to the vampire's taunting. It would do no good. Something was definitely wrong. He could feel it, but if he had the number-one suspect sitting in the backseat of his car, why was Elise not answering her phone?

Chapter 22

Elise blinked open her eyes, then closed them. The room was spinning and it made her stomach roll. When she opened them again, more fully, the bright light stung like acid. She quickly snapped them shut.

Licking her lips, which felt dry and cracked, she tried to open her eyes again. At first, everything was spinning, but she fought gagging so she could get her bearings. Finally, the room stopped swirling and she was able to focus a little on her surroundings.

She was in a small room illuminated by big spot-lights in all four corners. She was on the floor, hard cold tile, and there was something familiar about it. Rolling onto her back, she stared up at the ceiling.

Her body ached in all sorts of places. Especially her lower back and her legs.

Her limbs felt leaden, but she was able to lift her right arm. Blood streaked her skin. There were deep cuts on her hands and wrists. Staring at the wounds, she tried to remember how she got them. Had she gotten into a fight? With whom, though?

She licked her lips again. There was an odd taste in her mouth. Sour and strong. Almost like garlic. She swallowed the bad taste down and lowered her arm. She raised her other arm and saw similar cuts and bruises. Yes, definitely a fight of some kind.

She groaned from the soreness in her body. By the ache in her lower back she assumed she'd been lying on the floor for some time. But it was impossible to know how much time had passed, since there were no windows and no clock on the whitewashed walls.

There were pictures on the walls, though. Landscape paintings. She stared at them, a shiver starting at her toes and rushing up her back. She recognized those pictures.

Rolling onto her side, she surveyed more of the room. There was a sofa and chair and coffee table behind her, all mismatched and eclectic. She rolled to her other side and spied a TV set and bookcases. Next to them was a door. A blue door.

Swallowing down the urge to retch, Elise closed her eyes and opened them again. She had to be dreaming. This couldn't possibly be true. It was a joke.

Because if everything was real, then she was on the set of one of her first movies.

Chapter 23

Gabriel drove like a demon to the station. Once parked, he quickly escorted Diego up to an interview room where he sat him down and made him wait.

He leaned on the wall just outside the room and opened his phone again. This time he'd call Constable Sharpe. If Elise didn't want to talk to him that was fine, but he had to know everything was okay there.

The constable didn't answer his phone. Voice mail picked up after four rings. Gabriel disconnected and tried again, only to get voice mail once more.

He slid his phone into his pants pocket and stormed back into the interview room.

"Why were you at Elise's cottage this morning?"

Diego sneered, arms crossed over his chest. "I don't know what you're talking about."

Leaning on the table, Gabriel got into the vampire's face. "Don't mess with me. I know you were there. Why did you gut that wolf and leave it on her porch? Was it a death threat?"

That startled him and he dropped his hands to his lap. "What wolf? There was no wolf."

"So you didn't see a dead wolf when you came to the house?"

"No."

"So, why were you at the house?"

Diego sighed, realizing that Gabriel had maneuvered him into admitting he had been there. "I was just looking."

"Why?"

"There's no law against coming to call on a friend, is there?"

"It's called trespassing."

"I just wanted to make sure that she was okay."

"Why? I thought you hated her."

He flinched. "I don't hate Elise. I still… I still have feelings for her. I was an idiot for cheating on her. She's a remarkable woman." He smirked. "But then I guess you already know that."

"Yeah, I do." Gabriel leaned in closer, making sure Diego could see the anger in his gaze, and how hard it was to contain it. "And I think that pissed you off, and you went into the woods, killed a wolf and brought it back to gut it on her porch to teach her a lesson."

Diego shook his head. "That's not how it happened."

"Then tell me how it happened."

"I drove out at about ten. I parked on the side of the road. I was too chicken to drive right into the yard. I came across the yard and approached the house. I wasn't sure I'd be welcome, so I just walked around the house. And yes, I looked into one of the windows. And that's when I saw the two of you. So, I decided to get the hell out of there." He ran a shaky hand through his perfectly coifed hair. "I drove home, called Layla and asked her for a late lunch. I figured I should just move on."

"Layla would confirm all of this?"

He nodded.

Gabriel pushed away from the table. He believed him. "I'll need Ms. Lee's number to verify your statement."

"Fine. Got a pen and paper?"

Gabriel handed a pen and pad of paper to Diego. The vampire wrote down a number and handed it back to him.

"Jesus, you're just as bad as her agent. He's been in my face, too."

"About what?"

"About leaving Elise alone. He's a persuasive jerk, too. But that kind of crap doesn't work on a vampire of my caliber. I'm much too powerful to be swayed."

"Well, you should've listened to him and you wouldn't have been in this mess." Gabriel ran a hand over his face. He was feeling the fatigue but his anger and fear for Elise's safety drove him on. "You say you still have feelings for Elise. Have you been sending her love letters?"

Diego shook his head. "No. That's totally not my style."

Gabriel regarded him for a long moment, gauging him, taking his measure. However despicable he thought the vampire to be, his words rang true.

Clutching the notepad, Gabriel went to leave the room. "I'll need to check this out. You'll have to wait here."

Diego threw up his hands in defeat. "Fine. Could you have someone bring me some tea then, since I missed my lunch?"

That was when a tall woman in a three-piece suit barged into the room, her black leather briefcase swinging like a weapon. "This interview is over, Inspector. My client's rights have been violated."

"No problem, Counselor. Your client is all yours." Gabriel brushed past her and closed the door on her continuous stream of complaints and arguments.

As he marched down the hallway to the garage, he ran into Sophie. "What's going on?"

"I picked up Diego. He's not our guy."

"Are you sure?"

He nodded. "He was at the house but he didn't gut the wolf. He didn't send any notes, either."

"Are you sure?"

"Yeah. He's pathetic, but he isn't a sociopath."

"Where are you going?"

"Back to the cottage. I can't reach Elise or Ron. My gut tells me something's wrong."

"Okay, I'll drive," she said, turning around to join him.

"Are you sure?"

"Yeah, I'm a faster driver than you anyway."

"True." He tossed her the keys to the SUV.

A record forty-five minutes later, they were pulling up the driveway to Elise's cottage. The second Sophie put it in Park, Gabriel was out the door.

There was still blood on the porch and the front door was wide open.

Sophie withdrew her gun from her shoulder holster. "You take the back. I'll go in through the front."

Gabriel nodded and took out his own weapon. Senses on alert to every sound and smell, he skirted around the cottage and into the backyard. The first thing he noticed was the back glass sliding door had been shattered.

He mounted the steps to the patio. "Elise!" he yelled, as he crossed the deck to the broken windows. Gingerly, he stepped over the shards and into the kitchen. "Elise!"

There was no return call.

The kitchen was a mess. There were overturned chairs, and broken bowls and glasses. Tomatoes were strewn all over the tile floor. The scent of basil and vinegar laced the air.

Along with something else. Anger. Fear. And blood. Elise's blood.

There were droplets of it on the counter in the kitchen.

The sight of it nearly took Gabriel to his knees. He was faint enough that he had to steady himself with a hand on the table.

Sophie came into the room. "The front is clear. No sign of Elise or Constable Sharpe."

He nodded and walked briskly down the hallway to the bedrooms. Sophie followed him. He checked her room and the guest bedroom, where he'd put his stuff. He didn't expect to find anything. By the mess in the kitchen it was obvious someone had come in and taken Elise and she had fought back.

But now she was gone. And he didn't have a lead to who'd taken her or where.

They regrouped in the kitchen. "Call in the rest of the team. We need to go over this place with a fine-tooth comb. There has to be something here. There just has to be."

Sophie set her hand on his shoulder. "We'll find her, Gabe."

"How can you be so sure?" He had to catch his voice before it shook.

"Because I know you. You're a dogged son of a gun and you won't give up until you track her down and punish the bastard who took her."

She left him to make the call to the lab. As he stood there in the kitchen, looking over the broken glass and the blood, his heart thumped hard, painfully so, and he could hardly regain his breath. He hadn't been able to keep her safe. He'd promised her and then failed her.

Again. Fifteen years ago he failed to stop one of his best friends from assaulting Elise. He'd been late meeting her for a date and because his friend knew where they always went, he'd shown up instead, with malice on his mind.

He'd been late again. Too late in calling her, too late in realizing something was wrong. Too late to stop her attacker from taking her.

If she died, it would be his fault.

And if that happened, he was unsure he could continue on without her.

Chapter 24

Elise tried to regain her feet, but every time she moved, her head would pound and her stomach would roil. Her body didn't even feel like her own. When she tried to move her leg, her head would twitch. It was as if all her brain messages were going to the wrong places.

She'd been drugged. That much she figured out. But by whom? That she couldn't nail down.

The last thing she could truly remember was making a salad and calling for…

She couldn't remember who she'd been calling for lunch. Had it been Gabriel? Surely, if he'd been with her, she wouldn't be here. No, wait, Gabriel had left to go back to the city. So who had been on her porch?

She rolled over onto her side and tried to scramble onto her hands and knees. Maybe she could crawl to find a door to get out. At first her arms wouldn't agree with her legs. She tried and fell on her face twice before she was finally able to push up onto her elbows.

From this vantage point, she surveyed the room again, taking in everything she could. Trying to find any clue that could help her escape. She still couldn't believe she was on the set of one of her movies. Why would someone bring her here? Who had access like this? It had to have been someone she knew and worked with. Diego? She still didn't know.

Constable Sharpe. That's who she'd been looking for. The young constable Ron whom Gabriel had entrusted to look after her and to clean up the mess that had been on her front porch.

And that's when she saw the blood.

She was surrounded by it. Lying in it. It was all over her hands and her arms. It was everywhere. She was drowning in a sea of crimson. It was coming out of her nose and mouth.

Frantic, she clawed at her face trying to stem the

flow. It was coming out her eyes and everything was bathed in a dark scarlet hue.

She screamed until her throat ripped from the pain.

Chapter 25

"The rest of the team will be here as soon as they can."

Gabriel flinched a little as Sophie came up behind him. His mind had been elsewhere and he hadn't heard her approach. He nodded and ran a hand through his already messy hair. "Okay. Let's get the scene contained and mapped out."

"I'll get our kits." Careful to follow the same path she'd taken in, Sophie went back out the front to the vehicle.

Gabriel returned to surveying the scene.

From the look of the tomatoes and other ingredients still on the counter, he surmised that Elise had been making something for her and Ron to eat. The constable had probably been out cleaning the porch, as Gabriel had instructed him to do. There had been a green garbage bag on the porch, he'd noted.

Their lunch had obviously been interrupted.

Sophie came back in carrying both their crime-scene kits. She set them down in the living room, away from the scene in the kitchen. Most of the mess was in there, so it was assumed that was where Elise and/or Ron had been disabled.

Gabriel snapped on a pair of latex gloves and wandered back to look into the kitchen again. "The intruder must've come in through the patio door. Elise was probably in the kitchen, maybe had her back to the door." He glanced over his shoulder at the open front door. "Maybe she'd just finished making something and was going to tell Ron."

"The porch is partially cleaned. Ron must've been there then when the perp came at Elise," Sophie added as she glanced out the door to the porch.

"I can't see how one man could've snuck up on two people, both with lycan genes."

"Maybe Ron was taken out first."

Gabriel joined her at the door. "I don't see evidence of a struggle. Ron would've struggled. He's a strong lycan."

"Then something must've gotten his attention and

pulled him away. Because he would've definitely come running if Elise had been attacked."

"I'm going to do a perimeter search for him."

"Okay, boss. I'll start taking pics and marking evidence."

Gabriel went back to his kit, shoved some plastic evidence bags, disposable camera and plastic markers into his jacket pockets, and went through the front door. On the porch he looked around for anything amiss. It was hard to tell though since there was still wolf's blood splattered on the wood. He did notice three sets of footprints, though, in the blood.

One had to be his, one belonging to Sophie and the last to Ron. He crouched down to examine the constable's print. Then he followed them off the porch and around the side of the cottage. They stopped near the water tap and hose.

Ron must've been preparing to turn on the tap and hose off the blood on the porch. But he never got the chance.

Crouching, Gabriel inspected the ground near the tap. At first he saw nothing but fine, packed soil and a few weeds sticking out from the earth. But then he saw a darker spot in the ground. Squinting, he peered at it and recognized it for what it was. A drop of blood staining the dirt black.

He set an evidence marker down beside it and took a picture of it. Then he leaned down even farther and inhaled the rich, tangy odor. Everyone's blood smelled different. If he knew the person, Gabriel could distinguish their blood from another's. He took in three good whiffs and got Ron's scent.

Standing, he lifted his nose to the air and smelled, trying to pinpoint in what direction Ron had been dragged or carried or walked off on his own—which Gabriel highly doubted. The only way Ron had abandoned his post was if he was forced to do so.

After a few more whiffs of the air, Gabriel got a scent trail. He followed it across the field and toward the woods. Almost in the exact location that he'd encountered the paparazzi vampire's scent. The trail turned then, and continued down the tree line until it came to the road hidden by more trees and a fence.

Gabriel jumped the fence and that's where he found Constable Ron Sharpe. Dead. His throat slit ear to ear.

He cursed under his breath then crouched down to close the dead lycan's eyes. "I'll find him, Ron. I'll find him."

An hour later, Gabriel was back in the cottage with his team busy around him examining and collecting the evidence. He had Ron's body bagged and tagged, and it was now in the back of the SUV ready to be driven back to the city and to the morgue to have an autopsy done. It was obvious what had killed him—he was bled out—but what Gabriel wanted to know was how he'd been incapacitated to begin with.

"Gabe," Sophie said from near the smashed glass doors. "Check this out."

Gabriel neared where she was kneeling down. Her flashlight illuminated a clear liquid on the floor.

"What is it?"

She shook her head. "It's some kind of chemical. The smell is noxious."

"Chloroform?"

"No. It's something else." She took out a Q-tip and dabbed it into the substance. She then slid the Q-tip into a small plastic tube and capped it. She labeled it and handed it to Gabriel.

He set it into her crime-scene kit along with everything else they'd collected, bagged and labeled.

Looking at it all, he didn't know if it would help. He'd always believed in the evidence before. Always knew it would lead them to solving the case and getting justice for the wronged.

But right now he couldn't muster anything in his gut, any amount of belief or hope. He felt Elise slipping away from him. And he had no way of getting her back.

Someone patted him on the shoulder. Gabriel turned to look into Kellen's soulful eyes. "I'm sorry, Gabe."

He nodded, unsure of exactly what to say or how to behave.

"We'll find her, my friend. Believe that."

He nodded again, but his heart wasn't in it. Because everything inside him screamed of loss and failure. Already his heart was grieving Elise's death. And it hurt so much he could barely keep on his feet.

Chapter 26

Groaning, Elise opened her eyes again. After screaming until her chest hurt, she'd blissfully passed out.

She looked down at her hands and arms and saw that there was no blood. Lifting her hand to her face, she ran her fingers over her eyes and nose and mouth and found no sticky residue of blood.

It had been all a dream.

She turned over onto her side and looked around her, her stomach flipping over. No, not a dream. She was still on the set, on the floor, and she still felt raw and hollowed out and nauseous.

"It was a hallucination, Elise, from the drugs I've given you."

She startled at the voice. Pushing onto her elbows, she looked around the room, searching for its source. But she was alone in the room.

"Why..." Her lips were sore and cracked and her throat raw. She swallowed and tried again. "Why am I here? Why are you doing this to me?"

"You know why you're here. This is where it all started. Don't you remember?"

"No. I don't remember."

"You will. You will."

Elise rolled onto her back and closed her eyes. The tears rolled silently down her cheeks. She felt very alone. Where was Gabriel? Wasn't he coming for her? Did he even know where she was?

Chapter 27

Gabriel knew she was in trouble. He felt it the second he walked up the dark, deserted road to their rendezvous spot.

He kicked himself for being late. His father had kept him with another one of his lectures about how Gabriel was disgracing the family by carrying on with "that Leroy girl." He should've told him to shove his words. Then maybe he wouldn't have been fifteen minutes late meeting Elise.

When he came around the bend, that's when he saw her. That's when he smelled her blood and heard her whimpers of pain.

He lost it then. Without thinking, he ran toward

her. The only thing in his mind was to save her. He didn't even realize it had been Yves on top of her when he pounced on the man hurting his Elise. He hadn't known it was his best friend until he'd nearly ripped out his throat with one hand.

Leaving Yves to mewl like an injured puppy, he went to look after Elise, to tend to her. But when he looked down at her, she stared up at him, with milky-white dead eyes.

He'd been too late. She was dead.

"Elise!" he shouted. "Elise!"

That was when she sat up, blood dripping from her nose and mouth and eyes, and smiled. "You can't save me."

Gabriel jolted from his sleep. He knocked his head up against the car window.

Sophie glanced at him from the driver's side. "Bad dreams?"

He rubbed at his chin and face. There was a horrid taste in his mouth. He reached down and took a swig from the coffee cup in the cup holder. "Sorry for nodding off."

"You needed it."

Sipping his coffee, he looked out the window as they raced back to Nouveau Monde.

The evidence had been photographed, collected and shoved into stainless-steel kits. There was nothing to do now but to take it back to the lab in Nouveau Monde and analyze, study and try to find a connection. A thread to follow. Anything that would give them a lead.

The drive back was torture for Gabriel. Sitting in the passenger seat, he stared out the window and went over every little piece of evidence they already had. He went over every statement they'd taken from the people around Elise and tried to find the one thing he was missing. Because he knew it was there somewhere. It always was.

There was someone in Elise's life who had both the motive and the means to hurt her. It had to be someone close, to know her schedule and to have access to the soundstage, and know where her secret summer cottage was. Although it did turn out to be not so secret, as the reporter attested to.

But they'd been watching him and so far it didn't appear that he'd spoken to anyone about it.

So it was someone else. Someone they'd never suspect. Someone who appeared to be a friend to Elise.

Gabriel flipped open his phone and dialed. "Lily? It's Gabriel."

"Is Elise all right?"

"Why do you ask?"

"I get feelings sometimes. And this one is telling me she's in danger."

"Can you meet me at the station? I have some more questions for you."

"She's in trouble, isn't she?" He could hear the sorrow and desperation in her voice.

He ran a hand through his hair and sighed. "Yes."

"I'll be there." She disconnected.

Forty minutes later, Gabriel was in his office with Lily. The rest of the team was going over the evidence, pushing the lab to its fullest potential.

"I need to know everyone you've spoken to in the past week."

"Do you really think it's someone close to Elise?" He nodded.

"I just can't believe anyone who knows her would do something this awful." Tears still streaked her cheeks. She'd sobbed uncontrollably for a while after he'd told her that Elise had been kidnapped.

"I've been in law enforcement long enough to know that there are those who are capable of horrible, unspeakable things."

She just looked at him, maybe trying to decide if he was one of those people he was talking about. If he came face-to-face with Elise's kidnapper, he'd definitely find out just what he was capable of.

"I talked to Elise's publicist, Monique, and her gardener and housekeeper, to make sure that the house was being looked after in her absence." She squinted as if trying to remember things. "Rory called me just to see how things were going. I think that was in reference to Elise."

Gabriel frowned. "Rory is?"

"Her agent."

"Right." He recalled meeting the man at Elise's home. A vampire, if he remembered. And a seemingly nice guy. But hadn't there been something about him that had rubbed Gabriel wrong?

"How long has he been Elise's agent?"

"Going on ten years."

"He's a good guy?"

Lily smiled. "Oh, yeah, the best. Since signing with him, Elise has gone on to star in many great films. Before that she'd done only a couple of independents. Nothing too noteworthy."

"So, he's kind of helped her become the star she is."

"Most definitely."

Gabriel looked down at the files he had on his desk about the case. He flipped through the statements from the people closest to Elise, including her gardener and housekeeper. But there wasn't one statement from Rory Langford.

"As a matter of fact, it'll be ten years to the day come tomorrow."

His head snapped up at that. "Are you sure?"

She nodded. "Yeah, Rory's always been celebratory with Elise on their 'anniversary' so to speak. He sends her tons of flowers on that day." She sniffed. "He'll be heartbroken when he finds out she's been kidnapped."

Gabriel picked up his phone and made a call. "Francois? I need you in my office right away, and bring the reports from the vandalism case at Elise's charity ball."

It was no more than five minutes before the young male witch and analyst extraordinaire popped into Gabriel's office.

"*Oui.* You beckoned." He glanced at Lily, smiled and extended his hand. "*Bonjour.* I am Francois."

Smiling, she shook it. "Lily."

"Pleased to make your acquaintance."

"Francois, just give me the files please."

He bowed a little. "As you wish." He set the files down on the desk, then made himself comfortable in the chair next to Lily.

"The guest list from the party is in here?"

"Should be at the top."

Gabriel opened the file and rifled through it. He found the guest list and scanned it. He found Rory's name in seconds.

"Was every single guest questioned that night?"

Francois nodded. "Yes, as far as I know. All their statements should be in there, in alphabetical order."

Gabriel thumbed through the multitude of pages.

But when he got to the *L*s, there was no paper with Rory Langford's name on it.

"There isn't one for Rory."

Francois shrugged. "Everything should be in there. I made sure the constables had everything together before they gave it to me."

"Do you know the constables who completed the reports?"

"Good guys, good cops. All of them."

Gabriel chewed his bottom lip. Something wasn't adding up. Through all of this, all the investigations, there was one person who seemed to be exempt from everything—the questioning, the suspicions. Rory Langford.

That didn't seem right. Or normal. And his people didn't make mistakes. Something was definitely wrong.

"Have Rory and Elise ever been involved?" he asked Lily.

She looked shocked at the question. "Goodness, no."

"Did you ever get the sense that Rory had a thing for Elise?"

She shrugged. "Doesn't everyone? I mean she's gorgeous and kind and charming. Who wouldn't fall a little in love with her?"

"Do you need me for anything else?" Francois asked as he stood.

"Thanks for this, Francois." He touched the file on his desk. "And could you do a search on Rory Langford? He's a big movie agent, there has to be information on him somewhere. I don't care what it is. A parking ticket, an article in a newspaper, a Blockbuster movie rental card. Anything to get a bead on him."

"No problem." He looked at Lily and smiled. "It was my supreme pleasure to meet you, Lily."

"You, too." She fluttered a little like her namesake at his devout attention.

When he left, she sighed. "He's extremely nice."

"Who?"

"Francois. He's so charming. I bet he could charm a hungry man out of his last meal."

"Yeah." But Gabriel wasn't thinking about Francois. He was thinking about the vampire Rory. Could he possess some power that charmed people, persuaded them? Maybe even get them to do things they didn't necessarily want to?

"Lily, have you ever heard of a vampire with the power to persuade?"

"As in so charming you want to sleep with them at first glance?"

"No, like you'd jump off the tallest building in Nouveau Monde if they asked you to."

She shook her head. "That would be some power."

"Yes, it would." He scratched his chin where stubble was quickly becoming whiskers. "How old is Rory, do you know?"

"I don't."

"Okay. Thanks, Lily. You've been a big help."

She nodded. "You're going to find her. Right?"

"Yes. I'm going to find her."

She stood, reaching across the desk and taking his hand. "I believe in you, Gabriel. Because I know how much you love her. And I know how much she loves you."

He met her gaze and saw the truth there. His wall came crashing down. "Did she ever talk about me?"

"In a way. I always knew there was someone out there that she was missing. She never said your name but I knew, once I saw you two together, that it was you she'd been longing for all these years." She squeezed his hand. "Call me to keep me up-to-date. I'm going to go to Elise's and try to do something that will keep my mind distracted and the tears away."

"I'll call as soon as I know anything."

She walked to the door and put her hand on the knob.

"Thank you, Lily."

She smiled over her shoulder. "You're welcome." Then she left, shutting the door behind her.

When she was gone, Gabriel sighed deeply. He leaned back in his chair and closed his eyes for a brief moment. He needed to find out everything he could about Rory Langford. He didn't think he had enough to get a warrant for the guy, or for his house, but he would put out a call that he wanted to talk to him.

This guy was hovering just under the radar and Gabriel wanted to know why.

He had a bad feeling that Elise was in grave danger. That if it was Rory who had Elise, then she was under the thumb of a very powerful vampire. One who, if Gabriel was right, had been in love with Elise for nearly ten years now without any love back? Love could be a dangerous thing. It could create but it could also destroy.

He had to find Elise before that happened.

Chapter 28

Gabriel was heading down to the morgue to get the report on the autopsy of Constable Ron Sharpe, when Sophie caught him in the hallway.

"That liquid we found on the floor near the broken door?"

"Yeah."

"It's ketamine."

"Well, that's certainly not what I was expecting."

"I know, right. But ketamine has been known to work as a sedative."

"Yeah, but only in high doses. Where does someone get their hands on that kind of stuff?"

"Veterinarian practices use it all the time during

surgeries. It's especially effective with big dogs." She rubbed at her nose. "Something to do with the olfactory cells inside their noses. Would work effectively on lycans, as well."

Scratching his neck, he nodded. "Okay. Run with it. See if there have been reports of thefts at any of the veterinarian practices in the city."

"Will do, boss."

He grabbed her arm before she could dash back down the hall. "Oh, and keep the name Rory Langford in your mind. If there is a connection anywhere there, please let me know immediately."

She lifted her brow in question.

"He's Elise's agent. Has been for the past ten years."

"He's a suspect?"

"A person of interest right now. High interest though, if you get me."

"I always get you, Gabe." And with that she was out of sight down the hall.

He continued on to the morgue.

"Tell me something good, Ivan."

The medical examiner turned toward Gabriel, a rib cutter in his big hand. "Ron Sharpe suffered from blunt force trauma. But this did not kill him. He was dragged from one spot to another." Ivan pulled up one of Ron's legs. There were dark marks along the back of his thigh. "You see these are drag marks."

He set the leg down. "He was then bled out by a deep cut to his thorax."

"Any drugs in his system?" Gabriel asked, trying hard not to look at the body on the gurney. Ron had been a good cop and Gabriel felt he'd failed him in some way.

"I sent a sample to tox. Haven't heard back. Are you looking for something in particular?"

"Ketamine."

That lifted Ivan's bushy gray eyebrows. "Hmm, not a usual drug."

"I was thinking that Constable Sharpe was subdued with it somehow."

Ivan shook his head. "He was subdued with the bash on his skull I'd say." He pointed to Ron's head. "There is a substantial dent in it. I'd say he was knocked unconscious, dragged to wherever and had his throat slit. I would think he didn't regain consciousness after that initial blow."

"Okay, thanks, Ivan."

Ivan handed him his report. Gabriel took it and was about to leave when Ivan said, "Funny thing about that ketamine. I dated a vet once. She was an unscrupulous little minx, that one. She used to sell ketamine to junkies looking for a fix." He shook his head. "It's amazing to me what some people will shoot into their bodies."

"Can ketamine also be inhaled? Does it have to be injected into the body?"

"Inhaling it would be like sniffing laughing gas. Same sort of method."

"Could it act like chloroform?"

Ivan frowned. "In this way, you mean?" He picked up a piece of cloth on the table and held it over his nose and mouth. He released it.

Gabriel nodded.

"Absolutely."

"Thanks, Ivan." Gabriel pushed through the morgue doors. As he walked down the hall back to his office, his cell phone trilled. "Bellmonte."

"I got something." It was Sophie.

"I'll be right there." He slid his phone into his pocket and walked even faster down the hall to the analysis room that Sophie always used. She was sitting at one of the computers.

"What do you have, a break-in?"

"Nope, insurance claim."

"An insurance claim?"

"Yeah, after checking for thefts in the past week, nothing popped up by the way, I decided to just plug in Langford and veterinarian into the system just to see if anything popped up." She smiled. "Well, it did." She gestured to the computer screen.

On the screen was a long report, an insurance report claiming damaged and missing merchandise.

Reading down, he discovered the missing merchandise was ketamine and the person making the claim was Rachel Langford.

Gabriel didn't believe in coincidences.

"Sister maybe?" Sophie asked.

He shrugged. "Possibly. Does it say if she works for a veterinarian practice?"

"According to this, she owns this one."

"Is there an address?"

"Yup."

"Okay, let's go and talk to her. We need a connection. If there is one, we can get a warrant." He glanced at his watch. Time was going by too fast. And he feared Elise didn't have long. If his hunch was right, then maybe she was safe until tomorrow. Until the ten-year anniversary that Rory made such a big deal out of.

A half hour later, Gabriel and Sophie were standing the waiting room of Crescent Moon Heights Animal Hospital.

"Do you have an appointment?" the young receptionist asked.

"We need to talk to Rachel Langford."

"What is this in regards to?"

"Her insurance claim," Gabriel answered.

"One minute, please." The receptionist picked up the phone. "Ms. Langford, there are people here wanting to talk to you about an insurance claim."

After a nod or two she hung up. "She'll be right with you."

Gabriel and Sophie sat down in two available chairs. There was a Great Dane sitting next to Gabriel. The dog turned its head and rested it on Gabriel's leg. He petted the dog.

"He looks sad," Sophie commented.

Gabriel scratched under its big ear. "Yeah. I know how you feel, buddy."

The dog licked his hand.

A tall woman with long, dark blond hair came into the waiting room. Gabriel didn't need to be told that this was Rachel Langford. She had very similar features to Rory. They were definitely related.

After one final scratch to the dog, Gabriel stood and approached her. She smiled. "May I help you?"

Gabriel flipped his badge. "Is there somewhere we can talk?"

"Certainly." She led them down a hall and into a big office in the back. She gestured for them to sit in the two big overstuffed leather chairs. She sat down behind the equally impressive desk. "Now, what is this about? I have a feeling it isn't about insurance."

"Do you know Rory Langford?"

She arched one eyebrow. "He's my cousin on my mother's side."

"Are you close?"

"Not really."

"When was the last time you saw him?"

"Last month, at my mother's three hundred and fiftieth birthday celebration."

"What did you talk about?"

She hesitated and eyed them both. "What is this about? Is he in some kind of trouble?"

"I won't lie, Ms. Langford, but your cousin could be involved in a stalking and a kidnapping case."

She dropped her gaze and swiveled in her chair a little. It was an interesting response to his announcement.

"You don't seem outraged by what I've just told you."

"However much I don't believe he could be involved in something like that, there has always been something off with Rory."

"In what way? Are you talking about his vampiric gift?"

She flinched at that. "Rory has always been charming. Even as a child. But, yes, Inspector Bellmonte, he does possess a certain gift of persuasion."

"You mean you think he honestly has that mythical power of glamour? I've read about it in fiction books about vampires glamoring people, but I've never heard of a real vampire possessing it."

"Well, there's always a first for everything. And where do you suspect those authors, Bram Stoker be damned, got the idea for it in the first place? I'm sorry, no one is that original."

Gabriel nodded. She was probably right. "Would you know when he's using it?"

"In what way? You mean, on me?"

He nodded. "Yes. Could he have persuaded you to give him something? Something you think you've lost or never received?"

Her eyes widened. "Are you talking about my ketamine shipment?"

"Yes."

She worried her bottom lip with her fangs. "Hmm, I would never have considered that. But my supplier swears he shipped me the merchandise. I've never had a problem with him before."

"Would you be willing to give us a statement about all that you've told us?"

She nodded. "If Rory is using his power for bad then I won't be a part of it."

"Thank you." Gabriel jumped up. "Sophie, take her statement."

Sophie nodded and took out some official paper and a pen.

Gabriel flipped open his phone and called his favorite judge to get a warrant. They had enough now. They had just cause to search Rory's house and to put an APB on him.

Gabriel was certain that Rory Langford had abducted Elise and was holding her captive. He just hoped that he found her in time. Before Rory's warped mind went into overdrive.

Chapter 29

"What are you doing here?"

Her hand was shaking as she put it to her throat. Why she should be afraid she didn't know. But she was. There was no doubting it as her heart hammered in her chest.

He stepped into the kitchen. "What? I can't check up on my favorite client?" He moved even closer toward her. "Someone's got to watch over you and make sure you aren't making any big mistakes."

She shook her head, feeling confused and conflicted. Here was this man she'd trusted over the past ten years, but something was telling her that she didn't know him at all. That he was a stranger *to her and only now would she find out who he truly was.*

"Well, as you can see, Rory. I'm all right. Everything's fine. You don't have to be here."

"Fine." He shook his head. "No, I don't think everything is fine, Elise. You seem to be making some errors in judgment, I think. This Bellmonte character, for instance."

"What does Gabriel have to do with anything?"

"You've become too close to him. I don't think it's good for you."

"I will be the judge of what is good for me. And I've known Gabriel a lot longer than I have you." She took a step back from him. He was sweating and his hands were fidgeting at the pockets of his jacket. "I would like you to leave, Rory. I'll call you when I return to the city."

Smiling, he shook his head. "No, I don't think so. I'm going to stay for a while. You need me to be here, Elise. I can see it in your eyes. It's how you always look at me. Our love is so much stronger than all of this." He waved his hand in the air.

And that's when she noticed there was something in his palm.

"What love? We are business partners, Rory. That's all. Nothing more."

He frowned. "Now, now, Elise. You don't have to play coy. There are no cameras here. You can admit the truth. You can admit how much you need me, how much I mean to you." He stepped even closer to her.

She retreated farther, and cursed under her breath when her back bumped into the counter. She had nowhere else to go. "Rory, you've confused our relationship. I do care for you, but not in a romantic way. I'm sorry if you've felt otherwise."

He was still smiling. But it wasn't a warm comforting feeling. There was something unnerving and twisted in the way his lips curled upward. "That's okay. We'll have time to work that part out."

"What part?"

He pounced on her. She should've expected it. She should've sensed it in some way. She was able to get her arms up and push at him, but it wasn't enough to get away.

He grabbed her around the neck and pulled her in close. She clawed at him and bit down on his hand. But he didn't release his grip on her. He was strong. Stronger than she'd ever given him credit for.

He had her cradled into his chest, but she was still moving forward, dragging him with her. She struggled and kicked and made her way toward the sliding glass door to the patio. If she could get outside, she could get away and shift. He'd never be able to catch her then. No vampire could run as fast as a lycan in wolf form.

She swung her hands back, aiming for his face.
Her right fist did connect and she heard the distinc-
tive crunch of cartilage, but it wasn't enough. His
other hand came up over her face.

He had a cloth in his palm and it covered her nose
and mouth. There was some sort of chemical on it.
She could smell it. A strong, cloying odor that made
her gag. But she couldn't stop herself from breath-
ing it in. Her lungs needed air and she couldn't stop
them from contracting.

She struggled harder, kicking hard with her legs
and flailing with her arms. Glass exploded around
them, but still Rory held on. And still she breathed
in the chemical.

Her head was swimming. Her limbs were turning
leaden. Soon her efforts to get away were useless.
She could barely lift her arm. Finally, her vision
started to blur. Black spots spun around in her eyes.
She'd soon be unconscious.

After one final kick with her leg, Elise slumped in
Rory's arms and fell into a deep, drugged sleep.

Elise sat up and screamed.

Everything was coming back to her now. She'd
been in and out of consciousness for a while, but
now that she was awake, she finally understood what
had happened to her and why.

And who was behind it all.

The door to the small fake room opened and Rory

Langford stepped in, smiling. He was holding a bouquet of bloodred roses.

"Happy anniversary, my love."

Chapter 30

The judge had no problem giving him a warrant. And now Gabriel was in the living room of Rory's five-thousand-square-foot bungalow, tearing it apart, looking for anything to lead them to Elise's whereabouts.

He'd put out an APB on Rory, but so far no one had seen him.

They'd called his office and got voice mail, not even a receptionist. Gabriel sent a patrol to the office, but the door had been locked and no one answered when they'd knocked. It looked as if he'd closed up shop. An officer had asked around, questioned the other tenants in the building, but no one had seen Rory in a few days.

He had vanished. Right along with Elise.

Gabriel was convinced that he was the perp. They just needed evidence now to prove that theory. And they needed a thread to follow to find Elise.

It was past midnight. It was officially the next day and they'd run out of time.

Sophie came out of one of the bedrooms. "I got nothing. It's clean in there. Too clean, if you ask me."

"Keep looking. There has to be something. He sent her tons of letters. He had to have constructed them somewhere."

She went into the next room as Gabriel surveyed the living room looking for the spot to start his search. There was a coffee table with a drawer in it. He pulled it open and searched through the contents. Magazines. Copies of *Better Homes and Gardens, Men's Journal, OK! Magazine,* and *Time* were stacked together.

All the love letters had been constructed with letter cutouts from magazines.

He took out a copy of *Time* and started to flip through it, searching for any missing pages or cut pages. Nothing in that one. He picked up another. Again, every page was intact. He went through them all but one and found nothing. The last one was an old edition of *OK! Magazine.* There was an article in there about Elise.

Gabriel thumbed through the pages. Everything was in order until he came to the article on Elise. The two pages comprising the article had been cut and ripped apart. He spread open those pages, set them on the table and took several pictures. He then slid the magazine into an evidence bag and labeled it.

They had their first real evidence that Rory was the letter writer. But they needed more to ensure a conviction would stick. Right now, though, his main goal was to find Elise. Everything else would have to come second.

Standing, he surveyed the room again. There had to be something else. Something more. His gaze moved over the wall unit. On it were art pieces, a high-tech stereo unit and a long row of books. Gabriel walked over to them and scanned the titles.

He was of the mind that what a person read told a lot about them.

Rory had volumes of Shelley and Stoker. They were like history books to Otherworlders and not fiction, and he also had works of Shakespeare and Marlowe. And it looked like a lot of books of poetry. There was Dante and Chaucer, Lord Byron, and of course, Keats.

Gabriel slid out Keats and flipped through it. He

was familiar with some of his work. He wondered if this was where Rory had gotten his material for his letters. He remembered something from the last letter. It had been a poem, he was sure of it. And there had been something familiar about it. Something about scandal. And fame, maybe?

He flipped to the table of contents and skimmed down the list of poems. His gaze stopped on one— "On Fame." Gabriel turned to the stated page. And there between the pages were many cutout letters. Some of them fluttered to the ground like colorful confetti.

He read the poem. It was long, but his gaze zoned in on one part. It was the same as the poem in Elise's letter. *Gotcha, you bastard.*

"Gabe," Sophie shouted from one of the rooms. "You'll want to see this."

Taking the book with him, Gabriel went down the hall and into the main bedroom. Sophie was standing in front of a wide-screen TV mounted on the wall and a mahogany cabinet underneath it, with a remote in her hand. She gestured to the screen when he went to stand beside her.

On the screen was Elise, larger than life in one of her movies. It was one of her first films in which she played a battered woman. It was also the first film that she'd received many prestigious accolades for, the one that started her rise to stardom.

"This was already in the DVD player." Sophie paused the movie. "And if you look down there, there're all her movies, listed alphabetically and no other films. This guy is totally obsessed."

He glanced down at the lined-up DVDs then back up to the screen. He frowned. "Hey, play that again."

Sophie pressed a button and the scene played out. He recognized the movie. He'd seen it himself a couple of times. But there was something extra familiar about it.

"Wait. Pause it."

She did right at a moment where Elise is beaten into submission in the living room of her apartment. Blood seeped from her nose and dripped onto the tile floor beneath her.

"I've seen this room somewhere."

"Like, in person?" Sophie asked.

He nodded.

"Recently?"

He nodded again. He dug out his cell phone and placed a call. "Reginald? This is Inspector Bellmonte."

"Yes, yes, Inspector, what can I do for you? How is Elise faring? Can we get back to filming soon, do you think?"

"I need to know about the soundstages at the studio."

"Yes, what do you want to know?"

"Do you keep all the sets from movies?" Gabriel asked.

"Oh, no, that would be impossible. Do you know how many movies have been made here? Thousands. We don't have that kind of room."

"Do you still have sets from any of Elise's films?"

"Maybe. I don't know actually. Why do you ask?"

"Are there soundstages that are used for storage?"

"There's a prop warehouse on site. It would probably have some older sets and memorabilia from the sets. Hardly anyone ever goes in it, though. It's pretty old. I think they'll be tearing it down soon."

"What building number is it, do you know?"

"I don't, sorry."

"Thanks, Reginald." He flipped the phone closed. Sophie regarded him. "What's on your mind?"

"It's probably a long shot, but I saw this exact set the day we got the call to the studio. I went into the wrong building."

"You think he has her there?"

He shrugged. "I don't know. It's probably a long shot. Just seeing this movie in his player and seeing the exact set only days before." He shook his head. "I'm grasping at straws."

Sophie patted him on the shoulder. "What you need is some sleep. When was the last time you took a few hours?"

He shook his head. The last time he'd slept was

with Elise in her bed back at the cottage over fifteen hours ago. "I'm okay. I can go a few more."

"Gabe, I got this. I can sift through the rest of this stuff no problem. You don't need to be here."

He ran a shaky hand through his hair. "I've got nowhere else to go, Sophie. I need to be here, doing something, or I'll go insane. It's taking all I have just to keep it together right now."

She nodded and put her arms around him. "I know. I've been there, not knowing. It's hard to cope."

And she did know. Over a year ago, she'd spent weeks not sure if Kellen was going to live or die when he was in Japan undergoing medical treatments. Gabriel remembered how edgy and uncertain she'd been. Much like he felt right now.

She hugged him tight and then let him go. "Follow your hunch. I'll call you when I'm done here."

He showed her the book on Keats. "I'll bag and tag this and put it in my kit."

"Okay. I'm sure we won't be more than another hour, then we'll head back to the lab and try to put this all together. It's here somewhere, Gabe. The clue is in the evidence. It always is."

He nodded to her and took the book back into the living room. He closed his kit and set it by Sophie's. Without another word to anyone, he left the house and got into his vehicle.

He'd take a drive over to the studio. To check. Anything to get his mind off the horrible thoughts that raced there. Thoughts that he was going to be too late. Too late to save her, and too late to tell her that he couldn't go on without her. That he wished he could be with her every hour of every day. That a moment didn't go by when he wasn't thinking about her.

She was his everything.

And he feared he'd already lost her.

Chapter 31

"I will never love you, Rory, no matter what you do." Elise's hands were shaking as he got closer to her. She still felt nauseous. If he touched her, she might just lose it.

He smiled. "I'm sorry you feel that way, my love. But I think you'll change your mind soon enough." He set the flowers down on the table.

She tried to kick him with her legs. But he was too fast and avoided every swing of her foot. Besides that, she could barely move her legs.

Chuckling to himself, Rory reached down and grasped her by the ankles and dragged her across the floor toward the sofa.

He was so strong she couldn't fight him. If she still wasn't feeling the effects of the drug he'd given her, she would give him a run for his money, but as it was she couldn't muster enough strength to do anything but hang on as he whipped her around the room.

When he had her near the sofa, he released her feet. That was his first mistake; his second was thinking she was going to go along with whatever he had planned. She was no meek little mouse. She was a wolf, through and through, despite her recessive vampiric genes.

As he bent over to grab her around the arms, she lifted her head quickly. He probably wasn't expecting her to smash the top of her head into his face. She knew she'd connected. Could feel the spray of blood where she'd broken his nose.

"Damn it!" he yelled. He raised his hand and slapped her across the face. It was hard and fast and she tasted the familiar metallic tang of blood in her mouth.

"I won't make this easy on you, Rory. I will fight you all the way."

He wiped at his bloody nose and licked the rest off his top lip. Then he studied her on the floor, a trail of crimson on her chin from her split lip. "I never expected anything less from you, Elise."

She thought maybe she'd won a little victory but

it turned out to be short-lived when he reached into his pocket and pulled out a cloth. She didn't have to inhale the air to know it was soaked with whatever chemical he'd dosed her with before.

"You brought this on yourself, remember that."

She tried to pull away from him. She scratched and punched and thrashed, but he was too quick and too strong, and the cloth was covering her mouth and nose within seconds of him making the move.

She tried to hold her breath, but as her vision started to blur, from the chemical or lack of air she couldn't decide, she took in a ragged gulp and took it all in. Her head started to swim. It wouldn't be long before she lost consciousness. She tried to fight it. She didn't want to go under. It was a complete loss of control. And she hated losing control.

She hoped that when she woke Rory hadn't taken more than just her control from her. She could handle anything but that.

Chapter 32

Gabriel drove down to the studio. He got a call from the lab on the way. The tox report had come back on the driver who supposedly hung himself. There had been small traces of ketamine in his system. Because of that, his death was changed to a homicide instead of a suicide.

Rory Langford had a lot to pay for.

Gabriel hoped he was the one who collected on that payment.

He flashed his badge to the guard at the gate. He recognized him from his earlier visits. Chuck the security guard.

"What can I do for you this late, Inspector?"

Gabriel glanced at his watch. It was around two in the morning. Probably not a normal hour for people to be on the lot.

"What building is the prop warehouse?"

"Building twelve, sir." He handed a clipboard to Gabriel. Everyone who came through the gates had to sign in. As he signed, he surveyed the names before his. He didn't see Rory's name there. There were actually only four other names on the list.

He handed the clipboard back. "Not too busy here."

"No, sir. Hardly anyone comes this late. Sometimes the gaffers or grips will come to fix equipment, but most of the filming goes on during the day."

"Does the name Rory Langford mean anything to you?"

"No, I'm sorry, sir."

"He's a tall guy, short black hair, unusual gray eyes, dresses real sharp, vampire, drives a red Camaro."

Chuck shook his head. "Doesn't ring a bell."

"Could you check to see if he's been by the studio in the last week?"

The guard's gaze flitted left then right. He licked his lips. "I could get in trouble for this, sir."

"I know you could and I'm sorry about that. But this is really important or else I wouldn't ask. If anyone asks, you could say I grabbed all the reports from you and there was nothing you could do." He smiled a little at that since the guard was huge and lycan. There was no wrestling control from this guy.

He returned the grin. "Yeah, okay." He grabbed a binder from under the counter and flipped through it for the past seven days. He stopped on one page. He nodded. "Yeah, looks like he was by about five days ago at six thirty-three in the morning."

That coincided with the date of Elise's accident on set. It was another piece of the puzzle coming together. "Thanks, man. If there's anything I can do for you, let me know."

Chuck licked his lips again, looking like he had something to say. "Well, I'd love to meet Elise Leroy and get her autograph."

Gabriel wanted to yell right then and rip something apart. But instead he nodded, his lips tight. "I'll see what I can do for you."

"Thanks, Inspector." He pressed a button and the gate swung open. Gabriel drove through.

He got to the lot, which was huge, but unfortunately, he couldn't drive right to building twelve. He had to park near building ten.

He got out of his car and looked around. It was extremely easy to get confused here. Every building looked the same and if you didn't know what number it was, you'd never find your way. There were no maps to guide you through the maze of white stucco warehouses.

As Gabriel started walking toward building twelve, the hair on his arms and the back of his neck stirred. Stopping, he raised his head and took in a deep breath of air. Closing his eyes, he did it again. If Elise was close by he'd be able to scent her. But he didn't. He caught nothing but the smell of motor oil, stale goodies, doughnuts probably and coffee.

The coffee smell was fresh. Someone had been by here recently with a steaming cup of coffee.

He started to move again, but the sense of danger and dread wouldn't go away.

When he neared building twelve, he stopped again and listened for sound, any sound—a voice, footsteps, a scream. There was nothing but crickets.

He wrapped his hand around the door handle. It was locked. Using all the strength he had, Gabriel squeezed the handle in his hand. It snapped open within seconds, crushed by his fingers. Slowly, he pulled open the door, praying under his breath that it didn't squeak.

It didn't and he fully opened it and peered inside. It was dark inside, but he didn't need the overhead lights to see. He had good night vision courtesy of both his lycan and vampire ancestors.

He stepped into the building, hesitated for a minute and listened, but he didn't hear anything of importance. Looking one way then the other, he decided he'd go in a clockwise direction, searching every nook and cranny in the building. From his position at the door and the fact that there may have been an entrance on the other side, Gabriel crept to the left, intending to make it across the building in as little time as possible.

There was a path cut through the tall metal shelves of thousands upon thousands of props. He weaved his way around them, stopping every so often to listen. He heard nothing but his own labored breathing and his soft-soled shoes on the cement floor.

He was starting to think this had been a stupid idea, a desperate man grasping at desperate threads. He was wasting his time down here. He could be back at the lab helping analyze the real evidence. He could be out on the streets even, looking for anyone that had seen Rory in the past two days.

He was getting near the other side of the building, the place where they kept pieces of different sets. They were placed in an order, almost like puzzle pieces—a living room abutted a kitchen from a different era, old gas pumps sat up against the backdrop of space. He went through them piece by piece, but with every step his gut churned more and more.

What was he doing here? He was a huge fool to think Rory would take Elise here. There weren't even any rooms, just set after set. Rory would want privacy. A place he could have Elise all to himself. He wouldn't find that in a big old warehouse where anyone could come in.

He went through all the sets and was near the back door, the door he must've come in when he'd gotten lost the first time. Rubbing a hand over his face, he cursed himself again for wasting valuable time. He put his hand on the door handle, intending to open it and get the hell out of there. But something gave him pause.

He swung back around to the sets. There was something wrong. He surveyed the area, went back down a ways then came back to the door. Something was definitely wrong all right.

The set from Elise's movie was missing.

Chapter 33

Elise slumped over onto her right side as Rory settled her onto the sofa as if he was posing a rag doll. She was conscious but barely. She couldn't move her limbs much. Maybe a flinch here or there, but nothing that mattered. She couldn't push him away or strike out at him. And she wanted to with all her heart and soul.

He righted her again, but this time her head fell back. Luckily there were the sofa cushions to bolster the back of her skull. Her head was already pounding and she didn't welcome a knock on it to increase the pain.

"There you are. All comfy?"

She stared at him in shock. He was quite literally insane. She could see it in his gray eyes. It was as if he actually believed that she was okay with this, that he was entitled in some warped way to do this to her.

She went over the past ten years in her mind. Had she led him on somehow? Was there a time she'd ever kissed him or touched him inappropriately? She couldn't remember one incident. She'd never found him attractive. They had a business relationship and nothing more. She'd certainly cared about him, as one does with friends, but her feelings didn't go beyond that.

"You don't have to do this, Rory," she said. Though her words came out slurred and almost unrecognizable, she knew he understood what she'd said.

He sat next to her on the sofa and put his arm around her shoulder. "Smile, darling. We don't want to have a bad picture for our anniversary." He grabbed her chin in his hand and tilted her head forward. A camera flash went off from somewhere in front of them.

Elise swallowed the bile rising in her throat. He was taking pictures of them together, as if they were a happy couple in love. She pulled her head away, but he held firm to her chin.

"Don't move. You'll ruin the picture."

Another flash. Another picture taken.

He snuggled in closer to her, and his arm moved down, his hand becoming bolder. His fingers brushed against the side of her breast. She closed her eyes against the wave of nausea that washed over her.

"We met on this set, remember?" he said as another flash lit the room. "You'd just wrapped and I introduced myself over by the brunch table."

She opened her eyes and looked around the room. There had to be a way out. She scanned the walls. It was like being in a box. How had he gotten the set? Had he constructed it himself, making a room, her prison, so he could pen her up like a prisoner?

She had to get out of here. She feared for her life. For the first time ever, she didn't know if she'd survive. Her life was no longer hers to control. Rory had taken that from her.

Anger and hate and fear swirled around in her gut. She couldn't let him win. She had to do something, anything. She might not get out, but she was certainly not going to make this easy on him. He'd have to fight her long and hard to take what he truly wanted from her. Her soul.

"You were so beautiful that day. You still had the bruises makeup on your face. Someone would think that would've dampened your beauty. But to me it just added to it. Like a bruised flower, ready to be plucked and taken care of."

She let him keep talking. It distracted him so that she could figure out what to do. The drugs were still in her system, but she could feel the effects starting to fade a little. It would have to be enough.

First she flexed and relaxed her toes. Then her calf muscles, then her thighs. She kept at it until she could feel the sharp pain in her leg when she pinched herself. Her fingers worked, thankfully, but she was unsure she could lift her arms. She had to try it. But how without him becoming suspicious?

He pulled her tighter to him. She could feel the heat from his body and smell the sweet stench of gin on his breath. Taking a deep breath, she moved her arm. It jerked a little but it wasn't good enough. She did it again, and this time her arm flapped to the side and her hand landed in his lap.

He flinched, looking at her. She thought he'd get angry, maybe slap her for moving, but instead he smiled. "I knew you'd come around. You've been playing hard to get for too long now, Elise."

Then he did the thing she'd been dreading. With his lips parted so she could see his fangs fully distended, he leaned down to her mouth. "I've been dying to kiss you for so long. Other men may have kissed you before, but only my lips can possess you forever."

She made the mistake of looking into his eyes as he brushed his lips against hers. Although she was repulsed beyond reason, she couldn't find it in herself to pull away. And she couldn't look away from him. He drew her gaze in. She felt herself being drawn down a tunnel, a dark and dreadful tunnel. Her stomach roiled. She didn't want to go there. She wanted out. She knew she'd die if she didn't do something soon.

The only thing she could think to do was make a fist around the first thing she could get ahold of. His eyes widened as she crushed him. He shoved her away, and the motion propelled her onto the floor, but still she held on to him.

"You bitch!" he shrieked.

He grabbed at her hand, digging his nails into her flesh, and wrenched her hand away. While he was busy trying to breathe through the extreme pain she'd inflicted, Elise crawled away on the floor. Closing her eyes and gathering all her strength, she scrambled onto her feet and stumbled toward the closed door. She got her hand around the door handle before he recovered and came after her.

But he moved too quickly. She couldn't even open the door before he was on her, picking her up and tossing her across the room.

She screamed as she soared through the air. Her shins hit the edge of the sofa and she crashed onto the table, breaking it into pieces. Pain shot up her back and neck to swirl and boil inside her head.

Rolling over, she looked up into the face of death. There was no doubt in her mind that Rory was going to kill her.

Chapter 34

Gabriel stormed out of building twelve and looked at the other buildings surrounding him. Rory had moved the set, but he couldn't have gone far. It was here, somewhere. And if it was in this maze of warehouses, then Elise was in one of them. He was sure of it.

Rory was obsessed with Elise. And Gabriel found out that they had met on that set ten years before.

He believed that Rory had glamoured Elise into being his client.

Gabriel had to find out about these buildings and he needed help to search them. He got into his car and roared back to the gate to talk to the guard.

Chuck came out of the little guard office as Gabriel brought the car to a screeching stop, almost hitting the fence, and jumped out of the car. "Something wrong, Inspector?"

"Are any of the buildings empty? Or unused most of the time?"

Chuck's brow furrowed. "Let me check, sir." He went back into the office. Gabriel followed him in. He typed some commands on his computer keyboard. A map of the whole studio came up, listing all the buildings and their purpose.

He pointed to five different buildings. "These two are partially empty, only half of the space is being used, and these three are mostly old storage areas."

"Can you print that map off?"

He nodded.

"Do it. Print two."

Chuck pressed print and two copies came off the printer. While the maps printed, Gabriel made a quick call for backup, but they wouldn't make it here for another fifteen minutes. That was too long. So, Gabriel grabbed a printout and he handed one to Chuck. "I'm deputizing you, Chuck. I need you to help me search these buildings for Elise Leroy. She's being held captive by Rory Langford, her agent, the vampire I was asking about earlier."

Chuck gaped at him. "Oh, my God, are you serious?"

"Deadly serious."

"I'll do whatever you ask me to do, sir."

"Are you armed?"

Chuck nodded, and patted his hip. He had a Taser gun strapped to his belt. It would have to be enough. He couldn't legally give Chuck one of his weapons. A Taser would technically work on any species.

"I'll take these three buildings." He pointed to the two partially empty ones, and the adjacent one that was used for storage. "You take these two." He pointed to the other storage ones.

"Got it." Chuck reached under the counter and grabbed two wireless radios, handing one to Gabriel. "Turn it to channel two."

Gabriel did and tucked it into his belt. "If you hear or see anything, radio me. Do not engage on your own. Do you get me?"

"Yes, sir."

"Okay, let's go." He went back to his car, and Chuck got into the passenger seat. He turned it around and raced back to where he'd parked before. The buildings they were searching were behind the parking lot.

He parked; they both got out, and separated. Gabriel went to the left and Chuck to the right. Gabriel slid alongside the wall of the first building. He put his ear to the wall as he moved along to the door.

When he reached the door, he didn't bother to

check if it was unlocked or not. Waste of time. He pulled open the door and went in.

It was a huge cavernous building. It was completely empty. No offices, shelves, no props, no nothing. Just empty space. He didn't even need to bother going all the way in. He could see straight across the floor to the other door. Spinning on his heel, he exited that building and moved on to the next.

As he approached that building, the hair on his body stirred to attention again. Something shifted the air. Something ominous. He could feel a sense of dread all the way down to his bones.

When he came to the wall of the next building, he paused and pressed his ear to the cement. He waited a few seconds, sensing something amiss. He inhaled the air and caught a scent. And not just any scent.

Elise was here. He could smell her. And she was deathly afraid.

Chapter 35

Elise kicked at Rory as he came near, his eyes as gray and languid as quicksilver. Why hadn't she noticed their strangeness until now? They were both alluring and repulsive at the same time. One moment she wanted to surrender to them, and in the next she wanted to claw them out. Had he been glamouring her for ten years?

"Stop fighting me, bitch." He grasped her one ankle with his hand.

She kicked him hard in the head with her other foot, but it didn't faze him. He kept at her, making grabs for her other leg. She turned over onto her stomach and tried to crawl away, enough so she could gain her feet again. But he literally pounced on her when she did that and covered her body with his.

He pressed her down to the floor, his hands snaking around her body, his legs forcing hers apart. She bucked and writhed, anything to get him off her, but that seemed to just spur him on. She could feel his body growing hard and it made her stomach roil in revulsion. She had to swallow down the bile rising in her throat.

His hands moved up her body and cupped her breasts. "I've had dreams like this. You're exactly how I imagined you'd feel. Hard and soft all at the same time."

Elise reached up to his face and raked her nails down his cheeks. She knew she drew blood because she could smell it the second she opened his skin.

Grunting, he pulled his head back, but he didn't release his hold on her. "I'm stronger than you are, Elise. You can't beat me."

"I'll never stop trying, you bastard." With that, she rocked and bucked her body, and kicked back with her legs and pushed out with her arms. She mustered every ounce of strength inside her to get out from underneath him.

For a moment she thought it was working, because she could feel less pressure on her back. That was when she pushed up with all her might. But it was all for naught.

Rory lifted up and flipped her over onto her back faster than she could think. He covered her again with his own body, grabbing her wrists and holding them down to the floor. Her legs were trapped underneath his.

He smiled down at her, his eyes wide and intently focusing on hers. "Stop struggling. It'll be easier on you if you do."

Gathering all the saliva in her mouth, she spit at him in the face. "Damn you."

Grinning like a maniac, Rory narrowed his eyes and focused on her. She wanted to look away but found it difficult. His gaze was intense and mesmerizing. She felt dizzy and light-headed but still couldn't avert her gaze.

"I told you it would be easier if you didn't struggle. Now I'm going to have to remove some of your thoughts to make room for new ones."

"You can't."

"I can and I will." He grinned again. "I think clearing all your memories of Inspector Gabriel Bellmonte will do the trick."

Tears welled in her eyes. And even though she was disgusted and furious at what Rory intended to do, she still couldn't look away from him. He had captured her mind and she was powerless to stop him.

"Please, don't, Rory. I'll do whatever you want, just don't take that from me." The tears ran down her temples to drip on the floor beneath her head.

If she thought her tears and her plea would soften his resolve, she couldn't have been more mistaken. It seemed to infuriate him further. She could see the muscles along his jawline twitch as if he was grinding his teeth.

"It's too late to beg me, Elise. You are not the star of this show. I am. I am in control. I have the power," he snarled. "And when I'm done altering your mind, I'm going to kill your precious inspector. And it will be your fault." Then he laughed. "And the funny thing is you won't even care because you won't remember who he is. But I will and I can glory in that for the rest of my long life."

The tears just kept coming. She couldn't stop them now that they were falling. It was all she could do to defy him. She didn't have the strength or the will do anything else.

She'd lost Gabriel fifteen years ago, and she was about to lose him again. But this time it would be forever and not something she could undo or even regret.

She'd wasted all those years with anger and remorse, thinking she had more time. Every day that went by without Gabriel seemed like another day was next, that the possibility of seeing him sparked and then faded. But she didn't even have another day. These next few minutes would be her last, the last ones she'd ever regret not being at Gabriel's side.

"This will only take a moment, and then you'll feel fine. You won't even remember this." He leaned down into her face to catch her gaze.

She stared up into his eyes and wondered if it would be physically painful to have all those memories torn from her. They'd been with her for so long; Elise imagined they must've taken root fairly deeply in her mind. She wondered if it would be like weeding a garden, one weed at a time, like she did in her garden at the cottage.

Rory leaned even closer to her face. She could smell the stench of the alcohol he'd consumed on his breath and the sweat on his brow. And the blood streaks on his face from when she'd broken his nose.

It was the blood. The blood that finally wheedled its way through the mist in her mind.

Taking a deep breath, she screamed, "Gabriel!"

And when Rory flinched, breaking the contact of her gaze, Elise raised her head and sank her tiny fangs into his mouth.

Chapter 36

The scream pierced the silence around him, and Gabriel nearly dropped to his knees.

"Elise," he murmured. She was in pain but even more important—he knew where she was.

He ran full out to the next building, and as he did he forced the shift through his body. By the time he reached the main door he was all wolf. Grabbing the door handle in his powerful jaws, he tore it off its hinges and charged into the building.

The expansive warehouse was separated into various rooms. Gabriel raced down one corridor to the very back of the building. He didn't even hesitate before he was crashing through a closed wooden door. Splinters of wood pierced his paws and fore-legs, but he didn't feel it as he bounded into the room, savage fury turning his vision red.

She was there in the room, his woman. She was on the floor and the vampire was on top of her, clawing at her head. Blood soaked them both, but he couldn't be absolutely sure whom it belonged to.

Without another thought he sprang into action. He leaped over the sofa and hooked Rory around the midsection. He brought the vampire down to the floor, his claws sunk deep into his stomach.

The vampire stared up at him, wide-eyed, surprised obviously by his arrival. His face was a bloody mess, and it was then Gabriel noticed that his lips had been torn open. Movement stirred in his peripheral vision and Gabriel turned his head.

Elise was there at his side, on her hands and knees, blood staining her mouth and hands. Tears streaked her cheeks as she crawled over to where he had Rory pinned to the floor. The vampire wasn't moving much. He couldn't, not with Gabriel's vicious claws dug into his flesh. If he moved, he'd be gutted in seconds. Not even the most powerful of vampires could survive that type of injury for long.

"Gabriel," she breathed. "Oh, Gabriel."

He whined at her to let her know that he understood, that he was here. That he loved her with everything he was or ever would be.

She ran a hand over his body, tangling her fingers into his fur. "I thought I'd never see you again."

He snuffled her cheek once, and then when Rory moved beneath him, he growled and lowered his muzzle to the vampire's throat. He stopped moving.

Gabriel wanted to rip his throat out. Already he could taste the tang of blood on his tongue. This kill would be the most satisfying he'd ever had.

Elise gripped his fur. "Don't kill him."

Gabriel growled again and opened his jaw, scraping the tips of his razor-sharp teeth along the vampire's neck. Rory closed his eyes and whimpered like a coward.

"Don't," she murmured. "I want him to be alive to know that he will never have me. That I am and always have been yours."

Gabriel pulled his head back and closed his jaw. Turning toward her, he nuzzled her cheek again. He inhaled her scent. It relaxed him, and he was able to retract his claws from Rory's gut. He stepped off the vampire and moved to one side, his gaze still alert in case Rory decided to do something stupid—like move.

Elise wrapped her arms around his neck and buried her face into his fur. She was sobbing now, and in between sobs he heard her words. "I was so scared. I didn't think you'd find me."

He wanted to console her, to wrap his arms

around her and rock her in his lap until the tears stopped. But he couldn't, not in his wolf form. Closing his eyes, he focused on shifting back. He desperately needed to hold her close.

At the first shift of his bones, Gabriel felt movement next to him. He opened his eyes to see Rory rolling over to gain his feet. He was fast, this vampire, but the fact that he had to hold his guts in slowed him down. Enough, that Gabriel was able to bound after him. The pain was immense but he pushed past it. He couldn't let Rory get away, not after all he'd done. Especially with what he'd done to Elise.

Rory was almost at the broken door. Gabriel pushed off with his twisted back legs, half in and half out of his wolf form. He reached for the vampire. Reached and managed to snag a piece of him. Right across the face.

Howling, Rory slapped his hands over his eyes but still was gaining momentum out the door. But he ran right into two hundred and fifty pounds of lycan security guard. Chuck had his Taser out and he let it rip at Rory.

The electrical jolt dropped the vampire to the ground. He twitched on the floor as the current zipped through him like lightning.

Gabriel collapsed to the ground beside the vampire and finished his shift. It took him a little longer than usual but eventually he was back in his human form. He struggled to his feet. Elise was there helping him up, and she wrapped her arms around him. He could feel her tear-soaked cheek on his shoulder.

He hugged her close, stroking a hand over her hair, reveling in her, in her smell, in the feel of her body pressed close to his. Squeezing his eyes shut against the tears he wanted to shed, Gabriel breathed her in, heart and soul.

Words couldn't express the emotions hammering through him. So he remained silent and just held her, soothing her, consoling himself that he'd gotten to her in time. That he hadn't failed her. That he hadn't lost her. She was here, in his arms, safe.

Finally, movement behind him caused him to stir, and he turned to see Chuck and Sophie and an EMT milling about in the room. Rory was strapped to a gurney and was about to be wheeled out. Gabriel glanced at him one last time, and then he pushed the vampire out of his mind.

Sophie smiled at him and handed him his coat. "Here you go, boss."

He took one arm from around Elise long enough to slip the coat on. "When did you get here?"

"Five minutes ago." She nodded toward Chuck, who was busy putting his Taser gun back into his belt. "He called to let us know what the hell was going on."

"Thank you, Chuck," Gabriel said.

The big lycan shrugged. "I was just following your orders, sir."

"Ever thought of a job in law enforcement or crime-scene investigation?"

Chuck went wide-eyed.

"I think you'd be a good addition to the team."

"Thank you, sir." He puffed out his chest.

Gabriel squeezed Elise into his side. She hadn't yet let go of him. "Elise, this is Chuck. He's a big fan of yours."

"It's a pleasure to meet you, Chuck."

The big lycan blushed. "The pleasure's all mine, Ms. Leroy."

His arm around her, Gabriel moved toward the exit. "I'm taking Elise home."

Sophie nodded. "Okay, boss. I'll take care of things here."

Together they walked through the door and neither one of them looked back.

Chapter 37

Elise shielded her eyes from the sun as she stood out on the patio and looked across the field toward the woods. It was a gorgeous day and she never got bored of the view. For the rest of her life, she could stare out at the vegetation, the flowers and the trees.

Which was exactly the plan.

It had been three weeks since that night on the old movie set where she had thought she was going to die or, at least, lose the most important part of her life. But she still thought about it, still had nightmares.

She hadn't gone back to work. Reginald had been gracious and understanding about it and promised her that he would finish the film as is and it would be something she would be proud of. He'd called her yesterday to tell her it was done, but she hadn't had any desire to go into the city to see it. She probably never would.

The Nouveau Monde police had charged Rory with two counts of murder, her driver and Constable Ron Sharpe, one count of kidnapping and imprisonment, assault, harassment and vandalism. They had enough evidence to put him away for the rest of his long life.

Gabriel's last attempt to stop Rory from fleeing had taken his eyes, and ultimately his power. He was nothing now, just an empty shell of a man. Elise wasn't sure if he had ever really been a man. At least not a good one.

Sometimes she berated herself for not seeing it sooner. But according to Gabriel, Rory had one of the oldest and most powerful vampiric powers. Glamour. It had been used thousands of years ago to subdue a vampire's victim. Rory had used it to manipulate his way through his life. He had damaged many people along the way.

Lily had been a mess when Gabriel had brought Elise home. The girl slept in the chair in the hall just outside Elise's bedroom for three nights straight. Then Elise had told her she could move into the guest bedroom. Permanently.

Despite the Lily's lack of judgment with Diego, Elise trusted her. Enough that she left her affairs with her when she moved out to the cottage. Lily told her she'd hold down the fort until Elise came back.

She didn't have the heart to tell her that she wouldn't be back.

It was too hard. And those nightmares were still too raw and real. During the nighttime terrors, she would call out his name, thinking she'd lost him again, but he was always there for her, soothing her back to sleep, brushing away her tears. Gabriel had not left her side since that night and she knew he never would.

She turned to go back into the house. And there he was at the stove in the kitchen, stirring their dinner and talking on the phone.

When she moved into the room, he looked up and saw her, and a beautiful, slow, sensual grin spread across his handsome face. It made the butterflies in her stomach flutter something fierce. She put a hand to her belly and wondered if it would always be this way with him. Would he always stir something deep and primal inside her?

She certainly hoped so.

He flipped his cell phone closed and set it on the counter. "Dinner's just about done. Are you hungry?"

"Starving."

She moved into the kitchen and came up behind him to wrap her arms around him. He settled one of his hands on top of hers as he continued to stir the food.

"Was that Olena again?" she asked.

"Yeah. She couldn't find some form in the filing cabinet. She thinks my filing system sucks."

Elise laughed.

"So I told her to change it, since it's her office now and not mine."

He set the spoon onto the counter and turned around in her arms. Running his hands into her hair, he brought her head forward and covered her mouth with his. He tasted of wildness and nature and the spice he'd put into the tomato sauce he had concocted.

Soon kissing turned into caressing and the licking of her neck. She didn't mind. Gabriel could lick whatever part of her body he wanted. He was skilled with that appendage. And others, as well.

"Are you going to miss it, do you think?" she asked as he nibbled on her right earlobe.

"Miss what?"

"The job. Saving people."

He pulled back and looked at her, his fingers stroking her cheek and her chin. He shook his head. "I saved the most important person to me. As far as I'm concerned, my job is done."

She buried her hands in his hair and pulled him to her, brushing her lips against his. He smiled, then deepened the kiss. A flush of heat started at her head and went all the way down to her toes. The man could kiss, that was for sure.

She peppered his jaw with kisses, as she made her way to his neck and up to his ear. She licked his lobe and nibbled on the sensitive flesh there. "Turn off the stove," she whispered into his ear.

"I thought you were starving?"

She pulled back and smiled, lifting one eyebrow. "I am."

Gabriel whipped his arm around and turned off the stove, and then he came back around and picked Elise up, slinging her over his shoulder. He walked as fast as he could down the hallway to the master bedroom, where he tossed her onto the bed.

She laughed. "I didn't know you were so wild."

He stripped off his T-shirt and flung it over his shoulder. His fingers went to the button of his pants and had them undone and down his legs in mere seconds.

"I have a wolf's heart, sugar." Gloriously naked, he crawled onto the mattress toward her. "And it's all yours."

She wrapped her arms around him and pulled him close. "Forever?"

He grinned. "Absolutely."

There had never been a happier moment in her life than this one. She possessed everything she'd ever wanted in life. And he was all hers for the rest of it.

* * * * *

PARANORMAL

Dark and sensual paranormal romance stories
that stretch the boundaries of conflict and desire, life and death.

Harlequin®

nocturne™

COMING NEXT MONTH
AVAILABLE MAY 29, 2012

#137 GUARDIAN OF THE NIGHT
Vampire Moons
Linda Thomas-Sundstrom

#138 THE ENEMY'S KISS
Zandria Munson

REQUEST YOUR FREE BOOKS!

2 FREE NOVELS FROM THE PARANORMAL ROMANCE COLLECTION PLUS 2 FREE GIFTS!

YES! Please send me 2 FREE novels from the Paranormal Romance Collection and my 2 FREE gifts (gifts are worth about $10). After receiving them, if I don't wish to receive any more books, I can return the shipping statement marked "cancel." If I don't cancel, I will receive 4 brand-new novels every month and be billed just $21.42 in the U.S. or $23.46 in Canada. That's a saving of at least 21% off the cover price of all 4 books. It's quite a bargain! Shipping and handling is just 50¢ per book in the U.S. and 75¢ per book in Canada.* I understand that accepting the 2 free books and gifts places me under no obligation to buy anything. I can always return a shipment and cancel at any time. Even if I never buy another book, the two free books and gifts are mine to keep forever.

237/337 HDN FEL2

Name _____ (PLEASE PRINT) _____

Address _____ Apt. # _____

City _____ State/Prov. _____ Zip/Postal Code _____

Signature (if under 18, a parent or guardian must sign)

Mail to the **Reader Service:**
IN U.S.A.: P.O. Box 1867, Buffalo, NY 14240-1867
IN CANADA: P.O. Box 609, Fort Erie, Ontario L2A 5X3

Not valid for current subscribers to the Paranormal Romance Collection or Harlequin® Nocturne™ books.

Want to try two free books from another line?
Call 1-800-873-8635 or visit www.ReaderService.com.

* Terms and prices subject to change without notice. Prices do not include applicable taxes. Sales tax applicable in N.Y. Canadian residents will be charged applicable taxes. Offer not valid in Quebec. This offer is limited to one order per household. All orders subject to credit approval. Credit or debit balances in a customer's account(s) may be offset by any other outstanding balance owed by or to the customer. Please allow 4 to 6 weeks for delivery. Offer available while quantities last.

Your Privacy—The Reader Service is committed to protecting your privacy. Our Privacy Policy is available online at www.ReaderService.com or upon request from the Reader Service.

We make a portion of our mailing list available to reputable third parties that offer products we believe may interest you. If you prefer that we not exchange your name with third parties, or if you wish to clarify or modify your communication preferences, please visit us at www.ReaderService.com/consumerschoice or write to us at Reader Service Preference Service, P.O. Box 9062, Buffalo, NY 14269. Include your complete name and address.

PARA11

Harlequin® Romantic Suspense presents the final book in the gripping PERFECT, WYOMING *miniseries from best-loved veteran series author Carla Cassidy*

Witness as mercenary Micah Grayson and cult escapee Olivia Conner join forces to save a little boy and to take down a monster, while desire explodes between them....

Read on for an excerpt from
MERCENARY'S PERFECT MISSION

Available June 2012 from Harlequin® Romantic Suspense.

"I won't tell," she exclaimed fervently. "Please don't hurt me. I swear I won't tell anyone what I saw. Just let me have my other son and we'll go far away from here. I'll never speak your name again." Her voice cracked as she focused on his gun and he realized she believed he was Samuel.

Certainly it was dark enough that it would be easy for anyone to mistake him for his brother. When the brothers were together it was easy to see the subtle differences between them. Micah's face was slightly thinner, his features more chiseled than those of his brother.

At the moment Micah knew Samuel kept his hair cut neat and tidy, while Micah's long hair was tied back. He reached up and pulled the rawhide strip, allowing his hair to fall from its binding.

The woman gasped once again. "You aren't him...but you look like him. Who are you?" Her voice still held fear as she dropped the stick and protectively clutched the baby closer to her chest.

"Who are you?" he countered. He wasn't about to be taken in by a pale-haired angel with big green eyes in this evil place where angels probably couldn't exist.

"I'm Olivia Conner, and this is my son Sam." Tears filled her eyes. "I have another son, but he's still in town. I couldn't get to him before I ran away. I've heard rumors that there was a safe house somewhere, but I've been in the woods for two days and I can't find it."

Micah was unmoved by her tears and by her story. He knew how devious his brother could be, and Micah would do everything possible to protect the location of the safe house. There was only one way to know for sure if she was one of Samuel's "devotees."

Will Olivia be able to get her son back from the clutches of evil? Or will Micah's maniacal twin put an end to them all? Find out in the shocking conclusion to the PERFECT, WYOMING *miniseries.*

MERCENARY'S PERFECT MISSION
Available June 2012, only from
Harlequin® Romantic Suspense, wherever books are sold.

HRSEXP0612

SPECIAL EDITION

Life, Love and Family

USA TODAY bestselling author

Marie Ferrarella

enchants readers in

ONCE UPON A MATCHMAKER

Micah Muldare's aunt is worried that her nephew is going to wind up alone in his old age...but this matchmaking mama has just the thing! When Micah finds himself accused of theft, defense lawyer Tracy Ryan agrees to help him as a favor to his aunt, but soon finds herself drawn to more than just his case. Will Micah open up his heart and realize Tracy is his match?

Available June 2012

Saddle up with Harlequin® series books this summer and find a cowboy for every mood!

Available wherever books are sold.

www.Harlequin.com

HSE65674

Harlequin® Romance

A touching new duet from fan-favorite author

SUSAN MEIER

First Time DADS!

When millionaire CEO Max Montgomery spots
Kate Hunter-Montgomery—the wife he's never forgotten—
back in town with a daughter who looks just like him, he's
determined to win her back. But can this savvy business tycoon
convince Kate to trust him a second time with her heart?

Find out this June in

THE TYCOON'S SECRET DAUGHTER

And look for book 2 coming this August!

NANNY FOR THE MILLIONAIRE'S TWINS

Saddle up with Harlequin® series books this summer
and find a cowboy for every mood!